He had a way of reaching past her defenses, of making her yearn for things she'd learned better than to expect.

But even so, she couldn't pull her gaze from Devin, from the picture he made with their boys as they copied his long-legged stride, his shadow stretching past theirs like a promise of what would someday be.

She caught herself as she realized what that promise meant. Devin was a rodeo cowboy, the same as her ex-husband. Devin had left the circuit only for the sake of his son, and not long ago. That didn't mean he'd left forever. The temptation to lean on him might be strong, but she couldn't let the sense of security that came with having him around lull her into depending on him in any way.

But as Hannah watched Devin walk away, all broad shoulders and masculine appeal, she knew she couldn't help but fall for this cowboy dad....

Dear Reader,

Silhouette welcomes popular author Judy Christenberry to the Romance line with a touching story that will enchant readers in every age group. In *The Nine-Month Bride,* a wealthy rancher who wants an heir and a prim librarian who wants a baby marry for convenience, but imminent parenthood makes them rethink their vows....

Next, Moyra Tarling delivers the emotionally riveting BUNDLES OF JOY tale of a mother-to-be who discovers that her child's father doesn't remember his own name— let alone the night they'd created their *Wedding Day Baby.* Karen Rose Smith's miniseries DO YOU TAKE THIS STRANGER? continues with *Love, Honor and a Pregnant Bride,* in which a jaded cowboy learns an unexpected lesson in love from an expectant beauty.

Part of our MEN! promotion, *Cowboy Dad* by Robin Nicholas features a deliciously handsome, duty-minded father aiming to win the heart of a woman who's sworn off cowboys. Award-winning Marie Ferrarella launches her latest miniseries, LIKE MOTHER, LIKE DAUGHTER, with *One Plus One Makes Marriage.* Though the math sounds easy, the road to "I do" takes some emotional twists and turns for this feisty heroine and the embittered man she loves. And Romance proudly introduces Patricia Seeley, one of Silhouette's WOMEN TO WATCH. A ransom note—for a cat!—sets the stage where *The Millionaire Meets His Match.*

Hope you enjoy this month's offerings!

Mary-Theresa Hussey
Senior Editor, Silhouette Romance

Please address questions and book requests to:
Silhouette Reader Service
U.S.: 3010 Walden Ave., P.O. Box 1325, Buffalo, NY 14269
Canadian: P.O. Box 609, Fort Erie, Ont. L2A 5X3

COWBOY
DAD

Robin
Nicholas

Silhouette
ROMANCE™
Published by Silhouette Books
America's Publisher of Contemporary Romance

To my heroes, Dan and Nick

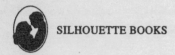 SILHOUETTE BOOKS

ISBN 0-373-19327-0

COWBOY DAD

Copyright © 1998 by Robin Kapala

Books by Robin Nicholas

Silhouette Romance

The Cowboy and His Lady #1017
Wrangler's Wedding #1049
Man, Wife and Little Wonder #1301
Cowboy Dad #1327

ROBIN NICHOLAS

lives in Illinois with her husband, Dan, and their son, Nick. Her debut book, *The Cowboy and His Lady*, was part of the successful Silhouette Romance CELEBRATION 1000! promotion. And her third book, *Man, Wife and Little Wonder*, was Romance's featured BUNDLES OF JOY title.

CODE OF THE COWBOY:

A *real* cowboy appreciates man and beast and land. He's strong, proud, hardworking. He can go it alone, but he knows his limitations. He can rope, rustle, wrangle...but he also respects. And the rough, rugged rangeland is a place he calls home.

As for the ladies...

A *real* cowboy knows how to court a woman. He's a guardian who'll protect his lady against all odds. He's a provider who'll make sure his woman has everything she needs. Most of all, he's a keeper. His word is his bond. And once he falls in love, it's forever....

Chapter One

Her sassy little dress swinging, dust settling over the tops of her black cowboy boots, Hannah Reese stopped outside the wide open door of a barn housing horses for Colorado's Greeley Independence Stampede Rodeo. From the brightly lit arena across the way, whoops and hollers carried through the night on hot, still summer air. The announcer boomed out the winning calf roper's name—Devin Bartlett. Hannah sighed in disgust. The event was over and it was obvious that despite the pass he'd sent her, despite his promise to pay the four months' worth of child support he owed her, her ex, calf roper Travis Reese, hadn't shown up.

Pushing curling black strands of hair from her warm face, her tangled ponytail clinging to the back of her sticky neck, Hannah fought the wave of nausea that came over her. A nausea she knew wasn't caused by the intense July heat. She pressed her hand to her belly and felt once again the life stirring within her— a miraculous life, considering her doctor had told her that Justin, now four, would be her last. The physical trauma she'd suffered from Justin's birth had—sup-posedly—left her unable to conceive again.

She *had* to find Travis. Their marriage might be over, but he had *two* children now who needed more support than she could provide boarding horses on the ranch she'd received along with the small settlement in lieu of alimony. Travis didn't know it, but she was ready to lay claim to that flashy bay roping horse he'd left at the ranch for her to take care of.

Her dark gaze swept the grounds again. There were cowboys and cowgirls over by the chutes, the bona fide kind, unlike herself. Travis had educated her in the cleaning of stalls and feeding of horses, but not much more.

A long lean cowboy was leading his horse her way, the reins loose in his hand, his stride easy, his hand-some face smiling down on the lanky boy walking beside him. They both had gleaming dark hair show-ing beneath their black hats. She'd once imagined Travis and Justin paired that way. Suddenly impatient with herself for letting her gaze linger on the man, Hannah turned to take a look through the barns for someone who might know Travis's whereabouts.

She found her way blocked by two glazed-eyed grinning cowboys.

"Hi, honey. You looking for someone?"

At the scent of alcohol Hannah wrinkled her nose,

which had become extremely sensitive in the past four months. She was suddenly aware that the bustle of activity around the barns had waned with the start of the steer-wrestling event at the arena. She wondered if that dark-haired cowboy and his son were still headed her way.

"Maybe she's just looking for a good time," the second cowboy suggested, swaying close to her side. Hannah didn't care for the glint in his bleary brown eyes.

"I'm looking for Travis Reese." Hannah swallowed the bad taste in her mouth that came with raising Travis's name like a shield. Her pregnancy made her feel vulnerable, even as it had her curling her fists in a surge of protectiveness for her unborn child.

"You're too late, honey." The first cowboy spoke, planting himself at her other side. "Travis got lucky last night. Pulled out of here, he got so lucky."

"Where to?" Hannah asked sharply, cutting off his drunken chuckle.

"The hell with Travis Reese." The brown-eyed cowboy leered down at her. "Looks like it's my turn to get lucky tonight."

With a sound of disgust Hannah gave in to caution and turned on her heel. The first cowboy gave way, but the second stepped in her path and matched his backward steps to hers, blocking and slowing until Hannah was forced to stop. She wished she could see past his broad shoulders to where the dark-haired cowboy might be.

"Let me by." She'd had her fill of this drunken cowboy. Had her fill of cowboys...

"Better leave her 'lone, Hank," the first cowboy mumbled from behind her. Hannah didn't put much stock in his ability to coax his friend away.

"Let the lady alone."

Now there was a voice that carried some weight, deep and firm with warning and filling Hannah with relief. Feeling suddenly weak-kneed, she stepped away from Hank, who half turned to cast a threatening look at the dark-haired cowboy. He only aimed an even stare right back, still holding his horse by the reins. The boy was still with him, his face as impassive as his father's, their eyes as gray as the shadows of the Rockies. The first cowboy pulled the second along in a face-saving gesture, mumbling again, this time an apology.

Hannah wiped her sweaty palms on her dress. "Thank you."

The cowboy inclined his head. He had long straight lashes over his smoky eyes, sharp features and full lips she imagined made women's mouths water when he smiled. But he was unsmiling now, passing the reins to the boy, who took them and walked toward the barn in response to some unspoken signal. Hannah wondered fleetingly about the sullen look the boy aimed her way when he went by, disappearing inside.

The cowboy stepped closer and, having noted the ropes coiled over the horn of his saddle, Hannah considered asking him about Travis. But the thought muddled with the lurking sensation that she was going to be sick again, the way she'd been that morning. Fighting back nausea, she drew quick breaths, and the white pattern on the yoke of the cowboy's purple shirt shifted dizzily.

He closed strong hands on her upper arms, and Hannah felt the heat and the brush of his fingers disconcertingly near her breasts. It brought everything into focus as if he'd waved smelling salts under her nose.

"Are you okay?"

"I'm fine. You can let go of me." Hannah stiffened her spine as the threat of nausea subsided. Couldn't these cowboys keep their hands to themselves?

He didn't let go. He looked down at her, his gaze flickering over her eyes, her cheeks, her mouth. She thought again that he was handsome, although his face bore the whiskery shadow of a long day. A fine layer of dust coated his clothes and he smelled of horse and sweat and baby powder.

Baby powder?

"Sorry if I offend."

"You smell like...*baby* powder."

"Got to keep the hands dry when you rope."

"I know that." She'd just forgotten. Travis had never smelled like baby powder, though, not even when Justin was a baby.

"I got in the habit of using it when my boy was small." The cowboy grinned down at her then, the curving of his lips every bit as devastating as she'd expected it to be. "Are you sure you're okay?"

Hannah narrowed her gaze. "I'll show you just how fine I am if you don't let go of me."

"I wasn't trying to take up where Hank left off." He dropped his callused hands slowly, but Hannah recognized the look in his eyes, the one that said he liked what he saw. "I just wanted to make sure you weren't going down for the count. You look kind of pale."

Hannah figured he'd look pale, too, if he was four months pregnant and had morning sickness that lasted all day long, but she didn't say so. So far, her pregnancy was her secret, mostly because she'd been too ill to gain more than a few pounds. And she'd thought Travis should be the first to know, if she could only find him.

"Look, miss, I couldn't help overhearing you ask about Travis Reese. So happens I'm looking for him myself."

"Why?"

"I might ask the same of you."

"I might say it's none of your business."

"I might say the same."

A standoff. Hannah debated inwardly. Then, considering this cowboy would likely come across Travis before she did, she told him, "I'm Hannah Reese, Travis's ex-wife."

That seemed to catch him by surprise, but he tried to hide it. Hannah pressed her lips together. He wasn't the first cowboy—or cowgirl—caught off guard by the revelation that Travis had been married, let alone divorced. The fact that it shouldn't matter anymore didn't stop the sting Hannah felt.

"I'm Devin Bartlett."

The winning calf roper, Hannah recalled. "Are you an acquaintance of Travis's?"

"We've followed the same circuit. I understand he has a ranch outside Greeley. Maybe you'd know where it is."

"I know all right. It's my ranch now. I board horses there."

He raised his brows at that, and Hannah didn't care for the judgmental look in his eyes. He was probably thinking she was some kind of gold digger, unaware like most that the ranch was heavily mortgaged. But all he said was, "Travis bought a roping horse off me a while back, but he never came through with the money. Any chance you know where that horse might be?"

Warning bells rang in Hannah's head. She didn't need to ask if the horse was a bay with a white star on its face and white socks above its front hooves. If Devin Bartlett took the horse and Travis failed to send child support, Hannah saw herself—her *children*— coming up empty-handed. "That horse is mine now. You'll have to take up your problem with Travis."

Having come to that decision, Hannah thought it best to forgo asking around further about Travis, certain, judging by Devin's stubborn expression, that she'd be in for an argument if she stayed. Ready to head home, she started past Devin, and for the second time that night found an unmovable cowboy in her way.

"That horse is a registered quarter horse, with papers to prove ownership, Hannah," Devin said evenly. "It never belonged to Travis, meaning it doesn't belong to you."

Registered? Hannah licked her dry lips, then stopped when the action drew Devin's attention. Damn Travis's worthless hide. He'd never mentioned the horse had a pedigree. On the other hand, a horse with papers was probably worth more than one without. Hannah squared her shoulders. "Like I said, that's between you and Travis. All I know is that the horse equals child support to me."

Devin pushed back his hat, his smoky eyes softening. Warmth flowed over Hannah, a sense of compassion she couldn't recall having known with Travis. But Devin's sympathy was apparently short-lived. She cooled abruptly at his stern tone when he told her, "The horse means pretty much the same to me. I train and sell horses to put food on the table for my son."

So, they'd reached another impasse, Hannah thought, gritting her teeth. Devin stood rooted in her path, his lean jaw jutting. Just then, the dark-haired boy walked out of the barn, snapping the tension when he said to Devin, "You ready to find that no-account Reese that stole our horse, Dad?"

Hannah let out her breath in a huff of disbelief. The boy only cast her another of his sulky glances. Hannah guessed him to be about twelve, maybe thirteen. His resemblance to his father was striking, except he had more dark hair poking from beneath his hat and he wore a black T-shirt emblazoned with a bucking bronco.

Devin only said dryly, "C.J., this is Hannah Reese. She was married to Travis."

Hannah almost flinched at the black look C.J. gave her. "She know where Jet is?"

"I believe the lady wants to see the registration papers before we get down to business."

How dare they talk around her like she wasn't here, Hannah thought, fuming. Did Devin give no thought to teaching the boy some manners? And she did *not* want to see the damn papers. "I told you, you'll have to discuss business with Travis. If you'll excuse me—"

Devin caught her arm, then quickly released it when she went still. "Let me check my duffel inside the barn for the registration papers. While I'm in there, I'll ask around about Travis."

Hannah wanted sorely to know where Travis was. Considering Devin wanted to find Travis as badly as she did and that he would have better luck getting answers, it seemed foolish not to stay around long enough to benefit from whatever information he gathered. But she wasn't backing down about the horse until she had the child support in the bank. "All right. I'll wait here."

"C.J., wait with her. And mind your manners."

Devin strode past Hannah. Inside the lighted barn he made a tall dark silhouette that had Hannah's heart beating hard in response. *Damn her weakness for dark-haired cowboys.*

Realizing C.J. was watching her with a far too knowing gaze, Hannah feigned disinterest in Devin to ask, "How old are you, C.J.?"

"Thirteen. Almost." He looked her over with eyes that reminded her more and more of his daddy's. Hannah wisely hid her amusement. Then C.J. turned her question back on her. "How old are you?"

Hannah did laugh now, though she fervently vowed Justin would never be such a brash young man. Fair play, she told herself. "I'm twenty-five. Almost."

C.J. seemed skeptical. "You don't look as old as my friend Cody's sister, and she can't buy beer yet."

Hannah sighed, and wondered how that could be. Sometimes lately she felt years older than she was. Better to change the conversation to something more pleasant. "I heard the announcer say your dad won the calf roping."

"He could be champion again if he'd stay on the circuit," C.J. assured her. He kicked at the ground with his scuffed black boot, seeming to talk more to himself than her as he mumbled, "He got this damn notion we had to settle down because of the divorce, so he's training horses now. We only get to a rodeo when he's got a horse ready to sell. He thinks I'd like playing Little League *baseball.*"

Hannah had barely gotten past the boy's swearing and the fact that Devin was divorced when C.J.'s disdain registered. Playing baseball was probably the dream of most boys, but apparently not C.J. "What do *you* want to do?"

"I want to stay on the circuit. If Dad can't get another place leased real soon to train out of, that's what we'll have to do."

C.J. sounded hopeful. Hannah couldn't keep her mind from spinning to the big empty horse barn at home, a facility she was more hard-pressed every day to support and maintain. She'd do anything to keep the ranch for her children...

Don't be foolish.

"So...you want to be a calf roper?"

"I'm going to be a bronc rider. My mom—she's a barrel racer—thinks I'd be pretty good. Dad bronc-rides sometimes, too."

Hannah thought it painfully obvious that C.J.'s mother was another reason he wanted to go back on the circuit. "Isn't bronc riding kind of dangerous?"

Devin's answer drifted from the barn. "It isn't as bad as bull riding, but I appreciate the concern."

Walking over, Devin grinned to himself as Hannah pressed her lips firmly. Pretty lips, pretty eyes, pretty hair, with her slender body wrapped in the pretty package of her loose flower-sprigged dress. Still, he wondered about her pale cheeks and the shadows beneath her almond eyes. She didn't look as if she'd been well.

She did look impatient, however, and Devin told her, "Some say Travis headed on over to Estes Park. There's a rodeo there around mid-July. I let it be known we're both looking for him."

"Well. Thanks for asking around."

"I don't have those registration papers with me."

"What a shame." The spark in her eyes said she didn't give a damn about those papers. Devin supposed he couldn't blame her, considering her concern about child support. On the other hand, he'd heard Travis had built himself quite a showplace after his finals win five years back. If the place was hers now, she couldn't be hurting too badly. Maybe, like his ex, Jolene, she liked to bleed a man dry.

Devin cast a glance at his son, thankful the boy couldn't read minds, then told Hannah meaningfully, "I'm roping here tomorrow afternoon, then I'll head home to Sedalia to pick up those papers. After that, I'll be paying you a visit concerning the horse."

A look of uncertainty quickly followed by wariness crossed Hannah's face, and Devin felt a flash of guilt.

But dammit, the horse was his. Training horses kept his son off the circuit, away from Jolene. She hadn't wanted the boy when she left a year ago, giving him custody of C.J., but recently she'd been down on her luck and making veiled threats that she would have her son—and money for child support. Devin wasn't going to let that happen.

"I'll take that to mean you plan on talking to Travis before then." Her composure obviously intact now, Hannah sashayed off, the skirt of her dress swinging. Devin's gaze seesawed between her black-booted legs and her bouncy black hair.

He was having a hard time imagining a pretty little thing like her married to a bastard like Travis Reese.

Hell, he couldn't imagine Travis married at all. But while it was bad enough for a man to hide the fact he was married and play around, it was beyond Devin's understanding how Travis could have had a child he didn't care enough about to speak of to his peers. Devin frowned a little as Hannah pressed a hand to her stomach, though she kept on walking toward a fancy red chrome-plated double-cab Chevy he recognized as Travis's.

"This ain't getting the work done, Dad."

Devin didn't have to look at his son to know those gray eyes would be full of disapproval at the attention he paid Hannah Reese. Since his divorce, his social life had taken a drastic decline, which probably accounted for the fact that he was more than a little drawn to Hannah. But the divorce had been hard on his son, too, even though C.J. didn't realize Jolene had counted herself lucky to be free of them. Devin counted himself lucky she hadn't taken C.J. with her.

With that thought Devin slung his arm about C.J.'s shoulder and turned back into the barn. And he tried his best to put Hannah Reese out of his mind—for now.

Hannah kept some kick to her stride until she reached her truck. Glancing over her shoulder at the empty spot where Devin had stood, she leaned heavily against the door she'd opened, dropping all pretense of perkiness. From over in the livestock building, the sound of the band warming up for tonight's dance drifted to her. Disappointment washed over her, and Hannah brushed it aside as deliberately as she did the dust from her flowered dress. She'd come here with the foolish notion that she might have ended up at that dance with Travis. She let go of that notion now with the liberating realization that it was the dancing she was going to miss, not Travis. It was time to accept that her marriage had been over before Justin was even born.

Giving one last glance in the direction of the barn, Hannah climbed into her truck. She knew the foolishness of lingering with the heat of Devin's smoky gaze burning her back as she'd walked. Even without that sullen boy of his to ward off women, a divorced woman with a four-year-old and pregnant with another child was enough to put off any man—and she wasn't looking for a man, anyway.

But as she drove home, Hannah thought she might be looking for someone to lease her barn. Maybe even Devin Bartlett.

What better way to keep his horse—*her* horse—in her barn until she heard from Travis?

Chapter Two

The night was hot, as only the Fourth of July can be. Hannah found it especially so as Justin clung warmly to her neck, waving a handful of pink cotton candy near her nose. The cloying smell of the sugary treat made her feel ill, but Hannah cherished the sweet feel of her son's arms around her. Returning to Greeley tonight for the carnival and fireworks as originally planned had been a good idea, after all. Justin shouldn't miss the celebration just because Travis wasn't here. So far, he hadn't asked about his father at all.

"I was right, wasn't I? You're having a good time."

Hannah's smile for her sunny-haired friend was prompt. Tilly was entitled to be smug. If not for Tilly's badgering, she wouldn't have come here and

Justin's dark eyes wouldn't be all aglow. "You were right. I hope Allie's having fun, too."

Tilly's pretty blond-haired blue-eyed daughter, Allison, was twelve, and Hannah had worried she might resent having to spend her night at the carnival with a four-year-old.

"Allie's having a blast," Tilly assured her. Tapping her white-booted foot in time to the live country music swelling from the nearby arena, her hands tucked into the pockets of her Wranglers, Tilly didn't look six years Hannah's senior. "She loves having Justin for an excuse to ride all these rides and play all those games she thinks she's too mature for."

Allie's motherly instinct, mixed with her tomboy ways, did seem to work in Justin's favor, Hannah had to agree. Even now, Justin was wriggling, wanting to be put down as Allie approached with tickets for the merry-go-round. Hannah settled Justin carefully on the ground, straightening the "Little Buckaroo" T-shirt he wore with his jeans and boots, realizing that her days of picking up Justin and carting him around would soon be over. She'd have to sit and hold him on her lap. And before long she wouldn't have a lap.

Brushing her hand over Justin's black wavy hair, Hannah was grateful for the impatient manner that indicated his only concern in life at this moment was getting to the merry-go-round. She pressed her hand to her queasy stomach, thankful, as well, that he'd finished his cotton candy.

Justin and Allie hurried over to select their brightly colored horses. The carousel started turning, causing

Allie's long hair to billow and Hannah's stomach to lurch.

"Hannah, are you feeling okay?" Tilly's blue eyes were full of concern and Hannah was tempted to tell her friend about her pregnancy. But Tilly would only blame Travis, and Tilly was already angry enough about Travis's not showing up last night. Having lost her husband to illness two years ago, Tilly had little patience for people who threw love away. And while her situation was half her fault, too, Hannah understood how Tilly felt. But she wasn't up to dealing with Tilly's well-meaning indignation right now.

"I'm okay." Hannah lifted her hair from her neck, aware it curled and clung in dark contrast to Tilly's sleek short cut. Tilly looked cool as sherbet in her skimpy peach-toned shirt while Hannah felt as if she was melting in her flared denim dress with its little cap sleeves. The glare of carnival lights against the black sky might as well have been hot sun shining down.

Cowboy hats bobbed through the crowd, making Hannah think of Devin, despite her best effort not to. Recalling the smile he'd worn for his boy as they'd walked from the arena after last night's win and C.J.'s obvious hero worship, she couldn't help wondering how he'd done in this afternoon's final competition. He'd probably headed to Sedalia for those registration papers the minute he'd roped his calf. Still, Hannah caught herself scanning the cowboys passing by for dark hair and smoke-colored eyes.

"Didn't expect to see you here again, Hannah Reese."

Hannah all but jumped out of her boots, whirling to face Devin, certain the motion was what made her heart pound and her head spin. He grinned, looking like the very devil in his black shirt, and she said tartly, "Back from Sedalia so soon?"

Immediately Hannah wished she hadn't reminded him of the papers. She hadn't mentioned Devin or their disagreement over the horse to Tilly, whose protective instincts tended to be overwhelming sometimes.

But unaware of the problem with the horse, Tilly was smiling appreciatively and curiously at Devin, who smiled in return, making Hannah more aware of her frazzled state and that Devin and Tilly were the same age, that Tilly did indeed look fresh and pretty tonight, that Devin was more handsome than she remembered. He didn't smell like baby powder this time. The clean smell of soap mixed enticingly with his natural male scent, unsettling Hannah in a totally different way than the smell of cotton candy had.

"C.J. wanted to take in the carnival before we left." Ignoring her attempt at provocation, Devin pushed up the brim of his black hat and nodded at Tilly. "Devin Bartlett, ma'am. I met Hannah at last night's rodeo when we were both looking for Travis."

Feeling as if she'd been scolded for rudeness, Hannah said hastily, "This is my friend Tilly Meyer. Tilly helps manage the neighboring guest ranch. She and her daughter, Allie, are here with my son and me."

Just then C.J. walked over from the direction of a concession stand. With the exception of his white T-shirt, which had the words "Cowboy Up" emblazoned across the front in red, he was a carbon copy of last night, from his scarred black boots to his moody expression. He carried a hot dog in his hand. Her stomach churning anew at the smell of mustard and grease, Hannah managed to say, "Tilly, this is Devin's son, C.J."

Coming to a halt beside his father, C.J. gave a nod and crammed half the hot dog in his mouth. Hannah swallowed hard, then closed her eyes, as if by shutting out the sight of the hot dog she could eliminate the offending odor.

When she opened her eyes, Hannah found herself under the scrutiny of three pairs of eyes. She gritted her teeth. The doctor had promised her the nausea would end sometime in her second trimester. Hannah could hardly wait.

"Is she gonna be sick or something, Dad?"

C.J. sounded appalled and Hannah almost laughed. She gave another swallow and willed the nausea away, grateful C.J. had downed the last of his hot dog. "I'm okay. I guess I ate too much barbecue."

"You hardly ate a bite." Tilly's blue eyes were suddenly speculative, and Hannah had to glance away. Having borne a child herself, Tilly was going to realize the reason for her recurring sickness before long. Hannah vowed to tell her friend soon about her pregnancy.

Devin's expression was as speculative as Tilly's.

But then, he'd had a child, too, so to speak. Hannah held his gaze squarely. She wasn't about to let Devin guess she was pregnant, not when she intended to wheel and deal with him about leasing the barn. If he saw her as vulnerable, the advantage would be his.

"How about I buy you girls a cold drink?" Devin suddenly offered. "I sold the roping horse I rode this week, so I'm looking to celebrate a little."

"Already got paid for the horse," C.J. revealed pointedly. Devin's look alone had him mumbling a second later, "No offense, Ms. Reese."

Thankful Tilly's attention seemed drawn momentarily to the merry-go-round, Hannah murmured a reply. But she suspected C.J.'s resentment stemmed as much from his father's invitation as from the money for the horse. That he didn't care to share his father was becoming quite clear. Avoiding her gaze, C.J. turned his belligerent stare on Allie, who approached holding Justin's hand and returned C.J.'s look with the frankness she'd inherited from her mother.

Justin dashed over to cling to Hannah's leg, making her teeter in her boots. She ignored the brief touch of Devin's hand on her arm, steadying her, and concentrated on Justin's bright-eyed pink-cheeked face. "Did you have fun?"

"I went round and round and round…" Justin let go of her to twirl, and Hannah caught his hand before he could make himself—and her—dizzy.

"Justin, I want you and Allie to meet Devin Bartlett and his son, C.J." Hannah was relieved when Justin stood with uncharacteristic silence, his dark head tilting as his gaze journeyed from Devin's shiny black boots up his long denim-clad legs to the silver trophy buckle cinched flat against his belly. Justin paused over that ornate buckle, and Hannah wondered if he was remembering Travis's shiny championship buckle.

But Justin said nothing, only completed his survey with Devin's smiling face. Justin smiled back, but his manner was unusually shy, and Hannah's relief fled, replaced by a mixed sense of anger and guilt to think that speaking with a grown man had become such a novelty to her son.

Devin crouched down to Justin's level, resting his elbow on his knee, leaving Hannah to look down upon his broad shoulders. Below his hat brim, the clean-cut edge of his shiny hair that brushed the collar of his black shirt had her curling her hands against an urge to touch. Sounding like one cowboy talking to another, Devin told Justin, "That was a championship ride you put on that red bronc over there."

"We got a real horse at home. His name's Jet. Mommy lets me ride him."

Hannah's heart warmed at the attention Devin gave her son, at the excitement it elicited from Justin. But as Devin raised his cool gaze her way at the mention of the horse, a chill worked through her.

"Sounds like quite a horse."

Hannah wondered if she was the only one who heard the edge in Devin's voice.

"Do you suppose you could handle another ride on that red bronc, cowboy?"

Hannah wanted to protest, but Justin was too quick for her.

"I want to ride the *purple* horse. He's faster."

"Maybe this young lady will take you over to try him out."

Devin rose and grinned at Allie, who good-naturedly agreed, accepting the money Devin dug out of his jeans pocket.

"Thanks." Allie looked to her mother for final approval before pocketing the money.

"Thanks," Justin echoed, leaving Hannah both pleased and stewing.

"You're welcome." Devin ruffled Justin's hair. Justin beamed and Hannah couldn't bring herself to deny her little boy a good time, although she would have preferred not to accept anything from Devin. And Devin knew it, too, his eyes glinting at her in obvious enjoyment of her silent pique.

"C.J., maybe you'd like to walk along with us while Hannah takes a break," Tilly suddenly offered, catching Hannah off guard. Hannah had had no intention of accepting Devin's offer to buy them a drink, but Tilly apparently misunderstood the look of protest she sent her, insisting, "We've got a good half hour before the fireworks begin."

"Why don't you go along with them, C.J., and have some fun?" Devin suggested.

From the black look C.J. sent her, Hannah knew leaving her alone with his father was the last thing the boy wanted. She had the urge to reassure C.J. that his father was perfectly safe with her. She had an even stronger urge to say she'd go with them and leave Devin to have his cold drink alone. There wasn't a doubt in her mind that Devin was arranging for her to be alone with him so he could badger her about the horse.

"Shall we meet at the barn to watch the fireworks?" Devin asked Tilly, who thought that was a *great* idea. As Justin pulled free of Hannah's grasp to go with her friend, Hannah felt bereft. She might have insisted then that she was fine and gone with them, but her stomach was churning again. She didn't want to be sick in front of the kids.

So she called to Justin to be good and silently wished Tilly luck as her friend set off with a reluctant C.J. trailing along. When Allie and C.J. drifted into step behind Tilly and Justin, Hannah cocked her head, wondering if the soon-to-be teens might actually enjoy each other's company.

"What the hell kind of name is Allie?"

C.J.'s muttered words drifted back to her and Hannah groaned. Beside her, Devin chuckled.

"The boy has a lot to learn."

"I'm relieved you noticed."

Devin's grin faded. "I'll allow I've let C.J.'s manners slip, but at least I haven't endangered his life."

"And what is that supposed to mean?"

"It means you've got no business letting Justin ride that horse."

Hannah pressed her lips. Devin wasn't wasting time bringing up the subject of the quarter horse. But his comment on endangerment couldn't be ignored.

"Are you telling me the horse—*my* horse—is dangerous?"

"Jet isn't mean, but he comes from racing stock. He's high-strung. It took a lot of patience to make a roping horse out of him. He's no mount for a child, or a woman—unless she's experienced."

Hannah affected a smile for a passing clown. She didn't know how to saddle the horse, much less ride it. Reluctant to admit her lack of knowledge where horses were concerned, suspecting that, like her pregnancy, the knowledge would only work to Devin's advantage, Hannah simply explained, "Justin was exaggerating. He only sat on the horse's back."

"Even that's chancy. It doesn't take much to set Jet off." Devin frowned. "Have you ridden him much?"

"I haven't been able to, with Justin to look after," Hannah hedged, striving for an offhand tone, silently vowing not to let Justin near the horse again. Thank God her pregnancy had kept her from giving in to her childhood longing to ride a horse. Aware of Devin's keen regard, Hannah added, both for good measure and to annoy the man, "Don't worry. I get along fine with Jet."

"Well, just don't forget what I told you," Devin grumbled. He turned them in the direction of the beer garden, guiding Hannah with his big palm pressed to her back. Her every nerve seemed to respond to the warm stimulus of his fingers, while she waited on edge for him to carry on with an argument over the ownership of the horse.

Devin surprised her though, asking, instead, about Justin. "How old is your boy?"

"He turned four in April." Right after Travis walked out, Hannah recalled, feeling the bitterness coil in her stomach.

"Justin favors you more than Travis," Devin commented, nodding to a couple of cowboys who sauntered by. Hannah barely noticed their interest, wondering why Devin didn't just get to the point.

"You're supposed to be relaxing." Devin moved his thumb soothingly against her back as he spoke, seeming to absorb and increase her tension at the same time.

Trying in vain to ignore Devin's touch, Hannah said frankly, "I figured you wanted to talk about the ownership of the horse."

Devin sighed. "I don't want to talk about the horse. I'm here to celebrate, remember? You could ask how I did in the calf roping today."

"Maybe I don't care," Hannah lied, certain he was going to tell her, anyway. When Devin only grinned, she said with exasperation, "All right. How did you do?"

"I won the go-round. That put me on top in the average, as well." He said it all without an ounce of swagger, which would have disappointed Hannah. Then he added, "That's why I feel like celebrating with my son, a beer and a pretty woman."

That caught her off guard. Then Hannah thought Devin might just get his last preference when a striking blonde dressed in snug red-white-and-blue West-

ern garb called to him from the beer garden. The
woman waylaid him at the entrance, wrapping her
arm around his neck and pressing a kiss to his lips,
while Hannah experienced the sudden feel of her hand
locked in Devin's grasp.

"You looked good out there today, Dev," the
blonde purred, leaning back, toying with Devin's collar with her painted red nails. Normally such glamour
would have had Hannah sighing with envy, deciding
to do something about her appearance. But her attention centered on her hand in Devin's as he loosened
his grip slightly, lacing his rough fingers between
hers, then holding tightly again.

"Thanks, Shelly."

"Some of us are getting up a line dance on the
stage over there if you want to join in."

"I appreciate the offer, but all I really want right
now is a cold beer."

Hannah didn't miss the calculating look Shelly sent
her way. And she wondered about the irritation she
felt as she watched Shelly slide her hand down the
front of Devin's shirt before the woman stepped
away. Being irritated with Devin was one thing; being
irritated by the attention another woman gave him
was entirely different. What was the matter with her,
anyway? She just met the man.

"See you around, then, cowboy." Shelly headed
for the stage, hips swaying. Hannah tried to tug her
hand free of Devin's grasp, but he was already pulling
her toward a table.

Devin got his cold beer and didn't blink over Hannah's request for a ginger ale. She sat with her hand finally free but still warm from the heat of Devin's palm. Despite her best efforts, Hannah couldn't resist a nod toward the group lined up single file on the stage, stomping and turning in time to the live music still booming from the arena. "They seem to be having a good time. I hope I didn't keep you from joining them."

"You didn't." Devin hardly spared the dancers so much as a glance as he lifted his hat from his head and hooked it over the post of his chair. "I like to hold a woman when I dance."

Hannah didn't know which entranced her more: the look in his eyes that said she was the woman he wanted to hold, or the fall of his glossy black hair over his forehead. She couldn't keep from wondering if he'd attended last night's dance, maybe danced with Shelly. Certainly C.J. would have done his best to keep his father away from a glamorous woman like Shelly, Hannah thought, curving her lips wryly.

Resting both elbows on the tabletop, Devin leaned in. "What brought on that smile?"

"I was just thinking about C.J.," Hannah said honestly, curious to see if Devin made the correlation.

Devin's grin was wry, too. "He keeps pretty close tabs on my social life." Then he sobered. "It was hard on C.J. when his mother left. It's been a year now, but he's still not ready to accept that it was what she wanted."

"He mentioned wanting to get back on the circuit," Hannah felt compelled to tell Devin.

"Because Jolene barrel races. Among other things." With that last revealing statement, Devin scrubbed his hand down his face and took a swallow of beer. He seemed unaware of his son's hero worship, but Hannah refrained from speaking of it. Devin's distaste when he spoke of his ex-wife was obvious, and his reason for leaving the circuit apparent. He wanted to keep C.J. away from Jolene.

"Does your boy miss Travis?" he asked.

"Sometimes I wonder if Justin even remembers his father. Tonight would have been the first time he'd seen Travis since our divorce four months ago." Hannah sighed. "I guess it's turned out for the best that Travis wasn't around much before the divorce, either."

Somehow, with those words, attraction sparked anew between her and Devin. His smoky eyes seemed to probe, to invite. Purposely Hannah sat back and reminded him, "I learned a good lesson. Marriage and rodeo cowboys don't mix."

Devin gave a nod of acquiescence. "I can't argue that."

That should have been the end of it. This feeling of desire for a man, for Devin, wasn't something she wanted or needed to contend with. But ignoring it wasn't easy when she could see desire for her glowing in his eyes. She was relieved when Devin broke the tension-filled silence and said, "You seem to be doing a fine job with Justin." Then he surprised Hannah even more when he murmured, "I've been cutting C.J. too much slack lately."

Trying to make up for things he could do nothing about, Hannah thought, understanding.

In that moment Devin didn't seem like the enemy. He was just another single parent striving to raise his son, harboring the same concerns as she. Hannah reminded herself that one of those concerns was to provide for their children. Devin was as determined as she, which meant he was as determined as she to keep the horse.

"Looks like my boy is in need of a little guidance right now," Devin said grimly.

Hannah followed his gaze to the entrance of the beer garden where C.J. stood eyeing them impatiently. Justin stood beside him, his dark eyes wide, his little mouth round with dismay. When she saw the pink imprint of a hand slap on C.J.'s cheek, Hannah understood why. Knowing Tilly wouldn't so much as step on a bug, let alone smack a child, she groaned, certain C.J. had met his match with tomboy Allie.

Hannah rose with Devin. He put his hat on his head, and she could sense his impatience in the touch of his hand on her back as he guided her toward the boys.

"What happened, C.J.?"

Hannah sympathized with the boy, faced with his father's stern countenance. She needn't have worried. Justin came to C.J.'s rescue with a heartfelt defense.

"Allie smacked him in the spook house!" Justin looked at Hannah in consternation. "Allie was holding my hand an' then the ghost jumped at us an' then C.J. kissed her an' then she smacked him..."

Justin ran out of air, but Hannah got the picture as C.J. rolled his eyes. Devin apparently grasped the problem, too, his lips pressing together in disapproval as he looked down at his son. Hannah understood his frustration, even as her heart went out to C.J., the boy now gazing down at his boots in the shadow of Devin's obvious disapproval, awaiting his father's wrath.

To her surprise Devin rested his hand on C.J.'s shoulder and bent his dark head near his boy's. "It generally pays to ask a lady before you kiss her, son," Devin advised.

"Hell—heck, Allie ain't a lady." C.J. shoved his hands in his pockets, lowering his head so that Devin had to peer under his hat brim to see his disgust. "She shot more targets than me, and she wasn't even scared in the spook house. She grabbed my hand and I...I just..."

C.J. shrugged then, shutting his mouth firmly as he sulkily looked up at his father.

Devin raised his eyebrows. "She grabbed your hand and you figured she wanted you to kiss her?" He kept the amusement from his voice, kept his eyes stern. But he couldn't resist a glance at Hannah. She'd caught her lip, trying not to smile, the same as he.

"I figured she might."

"Judging by the slap she gave you, I guess you realize you were wrong."

"Yeah, I figured that, too."

"Was Tilly pretty upset?" Devin asked, resigned to trying to smooth all the feathers C.J. had ruffled.

"Allie won't tell her mom—I don't think she will,

anyway. She just told me to get lost." C.J. shrugged again. "So I did."

C.J. looked miserable, struggling to remain offhand. As Devin's gaze drifted to Hannah again, he was thinking that pride always went first when you fell for a woman. "Son, you owe Allie an apology."

"You want me to tell Allie I'm sorry?" C.J. sounded horrified.

"I'd try cotton candy myself."

"Do I have to?"

"You have to make your apology. How you handle it is up to you." Devin felt the give in C.J.'s shoulders as they slumped in defeat. "You okay, son?"

"Hell—heck, yes. Allie shoots like a boy but she hits like a girl," C.J. said with disdain.

It wasn't what he'd meant, but Devin was satisfied with the lift of C.J.'s chin. "Take Justin with you and see he makes it through the spook house this time."

"Yes, sir." C.J. couldn't quite keep the grudging tone from his voice. Justin didn't seem to notice, enamored as he was with his new hero. Devin watched after the boys a moment, then turned to find Hannah's gaze on him, the warmth in her eyes catching him by surprise.

For a moment Devin simply looked back at her, fighting the pull he felt, a pull that was as much a connection between two single parents as it was man to woman. Shiny dark curls silhouetted Hannah's ivory face, her eyes soft with understanding. Devin fought the clench in his belly. Hell, even her eyelashes curled. The whole package that was Hannah

Reese was too damn appealing. He'd do well to re-member she was a horse thief.

He'd do well to remember, too, that C.J. wasn't ready for another woman in his father's life, some-thing Devin had forgotten when he'd given in to im-pulse and invited Hannah for a drink. Truth was, he wasn't ready for another woman in his life, either—at least not a ''settling down'' kind of woman like Hannah. If it wasn't for the problem with Jolene and his worry about C.J., he'd never have given a thought to leaving the circuit. He still wasn't sure he would carry it off. C.J. was as set on staying near his mother as Devin was on keeping him away from her.

''You handled that very well,'' Hannah noted, in-terrupting his thoughts with a smile.

''The boy gives me plenty of practice.'' Devin couldn't help thinking how Justin would test her someday, as well as how much harder it would be for her, as a woman, to handle things alone.

''Will C.J. be all right?''

''He'll be fine as long as the lady in question is forgiving.'' Devin tried not to focus on Hannah's mouth, tried not to appreciate the genuine concern he'd heard in her voice. ''I notice you don't seem too worried about Allie.''

''Allison Meyer is a little tomboy. She's always held her own with the boys, according to Tilly.''

Hannah's eyes sparkled with amusement and her lush lips curved in a smile. She'd barely taken a sip of her ginger ale, but Devin thought she seemed to be feeling better with every passing moment. She seemed to get prettier every moment, as well. Devin heeded the warning flash of heat inside him. "Feel like walking over to the barn now? I need to collect my gear."

And he needed to clear his mind, which seemed as muddled as if he'd been bucked off a horse and landed on his head.

"Certainly. I'm fine now."

Devin wished he could say the same for himself. He headed them toward the barn, refraining from capturing Hannah's small hand in his again.

But the night seemed to work against him, the sky full of stars, the carnival fading to a glittery backdrop as they walked.

The top of Hannah's head came just to his shoulder, and Devin looked down at her dark shining hair, at the thick curling strands spilling about her shoulders. The need to touch her seemed to consume him. Resolutely he pushed his hands in his pockets.

As they drew closer to the barn, Devin acknowledged another cowboy leading a prancing gelding toward a nearby truck and horse trailer, probably trying to get the animal loaded before the fireworks began.

Just then, a firecracker erupted, its sharp report echoing in the night. The cowboy's horse skittered and bucked. Hannah jumped back, coming up hard against Devin. He caught her arms from behind, felt the warm press of her body the length of his. He wanted nothing more in that moment than to turn her in his arms and kiss her. But Hannah was backing against him in real panic. Almost as if she was afraid of the horse.

The cowboy led the gelding on, calming the horse with his own unruffled manner. Hannah drew a steadying breath and Devin swore he could feel her pulse drum against his fingers where he'd curled his hands about her bare arms.

Devin did turn her in his arms then, but he refrained from kissing her, asking, instead, "You okay?"

"Of course, I am. That firecracker gave me a start, that's all." Hannah pulled free and resumed walking toward the barn.

Devin hesitated a moment. Then he followed her into the barn. Any person might have reacted the same to a suddenly bucking horse.

The problem was, Devin thought, Hannah didn't have the toughness of a woman who'd spent time on the rodeo circuit. She had a softness about her that made a man assume she needed protection; made him assume she couldn't know her way around a horse despite the fact he *knew* she was handling *his* high-strung horse. At least she'd said she was.

They reached the empty stall he'd used for the horse he'd sold, but Devin noticed that the handsome sorrel in the next stall caught Hannah's eye as it came up to the door for attention. "He belongs to a friend of mine."

"He's beautiful."

Coiling the rope he'd picked up, Devin urged, "Go on and pet him. He's real gentle and Charlie won't mind."

"If you're sure he won't mind…"

Did she mean Charlie or the horse, Devin wondered as Hannah moved slowly closer to stroke the sorrel's nose. Something in the cautious way she approached the horse had him ask, "How'd you come to be married to Travis Reese?"

Hannah went on petting the horse's nose. Devin was surprised. As a rule, horses didn't like their noses petted, but it was clear this horse didn't mind.

"I met him during the January rodeo in Denver, just after he won the calf-roping championship at the National Finals Rodeo in Las Vegas. He started coming into my father's café where I worked, and he kept coming back whenever he was passing through. We were married in July and by the end of summer I was pregnant with Justin..."

Her voice trailed off, and Devin suspected Hannah's marriage had been all downhill after her pregnancy. It was clear that Travis, a rugged rodeo champion, had swept a young Hannah right off her feet. Then Reese had left her to cope with child rearing alone.

Which explained why she was determined to have his horse, why he felt this bond with her despite that.

Devin watched as Hannah drew back her hand from the sorrel. She started to lay her palm against her stomach, the way he'd seen her do last night, then she curled her fingers uncertainly. She didn't seem to know what to do with that small soft hand, so Devin reached out and took it in his.

Standing beside her, he raised their clasped hands to a spot on the compliant horse's neck, near its ear, where he held her palm pressed to the sorrel's warm silky coat. ''They like being petted here, where their mamas nuzzle them as colts.''

''I know that,'' Hannah said quickly, her glance dark with a wariness that had him tightening his hold on her hand when he should have let go. He hadn't intended to touch her again. But the barn lights were low and the carnival and crowd seemed far away. Hannah's scent came over him, seductive as silk, enfolding him until he had no thought but her.

Outside, another firecracker went off. The sorrel snorted, but held its ground. This time, when Hannah jolted, jerking back her hand, there was no mistaking that her fear was of the horse.

Devin kept hold of Hannah's hand. Five years with a pro cowboy like Reese, and despite her adulation of horses, Hannah was afraid of them. Didn't say much for Travis, Devin thought. He turned her by the shoulder to face him and felt her shiver beneath his hand. Horses weren't the only thing she was skittish around. That didn't say much for Travis, either.

''You don't have to be afraid.''

''I'm not afraid.'' Tension traveled a hot circuit from her body to his hands, but she didn't pull away, as if to back up her words.

Devin inched closer. ''Didn't Travis teach you anything about horses?''

''I know how to take care of Jet, if you're implying differently.''

''Be careful around that horse,'' he warned her again, but softly, letting the words ease past her defensive manner, the same way he'd get his point across to a distrustful horse.

"I can handle him."

"If you say so." That brief flicker in her eyes said she was lying. He didn't know why, and worse yet, looking down at her glowing face, the deep darkness in her eyes, the unconscious parting of her lips, he didn't care. Not even thoughts of C.J. or of self-preservation made him care, kept him from taking the step that had his body lightly brushing hers. Hannah's eyes widened, but she didn't step away. With the warmth and awareness of that slight contact still rocking through him, Devin leaned down and kissed Hannah's sweet full lips.

He thought her lips moved beneath his, thought maybe the earth shifted beneath his boots. But he wasn't so sure a second later when Hannah jerked free and slapped him.

"How dare you!" Hannah's breasts heaved with her indignation, her lips and cheeks rosy now.

Devin rubbed his stinging cheek with his palm, almost willing to dare again. But he hadn't stolen that kiss. His intentions had been clear. So he challenged, "How dare I what?"

"*Kiss* me."

Devin bit back a grin. There was more fire in Hannah's eyes than in a Fourth of July sparkler. "Felt to me like you kissed me back."

"You just caught me unawares."

If he had, he wanted to do it again. But, wiser now, Devin kept his hands to himself. "Can you tell me straight out that you didn't know I wanted to kiss you?''

Hannah's gaze strayed briefly from his. He knew she wouldn't even get the lie out this time. ''Maybe I knew you wanted to kiss me.'' Then she fixed him with a self-righteous stare. ''That doesn't mean I thought you'd actually do it.''

He shouldn't have, Devin agreed, but before he could concede his mistake, Hannah said huffily, ''Small wonder your son doesn't know the proper way to treat a lady.''

Devin felt his first flare of temper. ''Let's leave my son out of this.''

Then he saw it was too late for that, for C.J. stood watching them from the barn door. For how long, Devin didn't know, but judging by the look of disgust on C.J.'s face, it had been long enough to have seen him kiss Hannah. Long enough to have seen him get slapped, Devin thought ruefully.

With her realization of C.J.'s presence, Hannah's cheeks reddened. Devin sighed as she turned on her heel and walked out of the barn with a brief nod to C.J., who offered no response. As C.J. stalked over to him, Devin noted the sticks of cotton candy his son held in each hand.

''I got this for Allie. She's waiting outside for the fireworks to start.'' That C.J. was angry about the kiss was plain.

Devin struggled momentarily with his temper. But duty to his son won out. He told himself there would be other women, better nights to pursue them. Somehow the thought didn't prove uplifting. "Guess I'd better load our gear. We've got a long ride home yet tonight."

"Thought maybe you figured on staying another night." C.J. was trying to sound unconcerned, but Devin recognized the insecurity in C.J.'s voice that told him his son feared he would stay, feared he had taken a serious liking to Hannah Reese.

Knowing C.J. wasn't ready for that any more than he was ready to accept that it was over between him and Jolene, Devin slung his arm across C.J.'s shoulders. "I think we've caused enough trouble in this town for tonight."

"We still going to watch those fireworks?"

"Well, we told the ladies we would. It wouldn't be polite to walk out on them."

Devin felt the war waging inside C.J. as the boy's shoulders tensed. C.J. wanted to stay for the girl, Allie, as much he didn't want Devin to stay for Hannah. His son was coming to understand the ways of life, but not with the same freedom and joy as other kids whose families were whole. Guilt rolled over Devin, then relief, when C.J. grudgingly held out a stick of cotton candy.

"Guess you better take one of these if we're staying."

"Thanks. This will help keep the peace until we head home."

They watched the fireworks then. And Devin struggled with the fire within him as color exploded in the black sky and rained over Hannah, holding her cotton candy, while his son stood stoically beside him.

Chapter Three

Taking a break from her morning chores, Hannah leaned in the barn doorway, savoring the breeze, which carried a hint of the distant snow-capped mountains. Inside, Jet swished through a clean bed of straw. Hannah could hear Justin talking to the animal, and she smiled at the idea of her son growing up on the open plain, sharing her love of horses.

She wanted to give Justin *everything*. And with fear of losing the ranch heavy on her mind, Hannah thought she understood more than ever how it must have hurt her parents to have been unable to give her the horse she'd longed for as a girl.

Hannah rested her hand on her belly, her stomach somewhat settled since her initial morning sickness. She knew it would be easier to call it quits here and go back to Denver. She could get out from under the mortgage, go back to work in her parents' modest café, secure in her future.

There were days she was tempted. When the bills came, when caring for Justin, the ranch and herself seemed overwhelming.

But she saw this ranch as a means to give her children a life they might only have dreamed of. Hannah's gaze drifted to the sprawling white ranch house. The border of delicate blue-violet columbine she'd planted had spread the length of the wraparound porch. She'd taken root the same as those flowers. She wasn't going to lose the home she'd made here, even if it meant leasing the barn to Devin Bartlett.

He shouldn't have kissed her.

But despite her pique with Devin two nights ago, Hannah found herself replaying his kiss in her mind yet again. It had been wonderful, from the enticing brush of his tall lean body, to the firm, warm press of his lips upon hers. For a moment, she'd kissed him back. He'd made her forget everything: Travis, worries about the ranch, even Justin.

A kiss was not what she needed from Devin. It was probably foolish to let that cowboy in the vicinity of her mending heart. But with a mortgage payment due, she'd have leased the barn to the devil himself to get the money she needed. In this case, the devil was a handsome cowboy, Devin Bartlett.

The breeze died down, leaving the plains to bake in hot summer sun. Hannah pushed up the sleeves of the pale denim shirt she wore over jeans unsnapped at the waist to accommodate the baby she carried. Her pregnancy and Devin's resentful son were enough to check any desire Devin might feel for her. The real problem, she knew, lay in her own foolish heart.

She didn't doubt Devin would eventually show up for his horse, and when he did, she meant to do business over both the horse *and* a lease. If the worst happened and she was left empty-handed, she'd just keep after Travis for child support and lease the barn to someone else. Yet the chances of collecting from Travis didn't look good, and the thought of having some strange cowboy working at the ranch around her and her son had little appeal, coming on the heels of that run-in with that cowboy Hank at the fair. She realized, at least in one respect, she trusted Devin.

A squeak and rattle from behind made her turn. Justin was pulling his hay-filled red wagon along, spilling bits of chaff over her freshly swept aisle. Her lips curving wryly, she knew that the cuffs she'd rolled up on Justin's jeans would be collecting chaff, too. He scuffed along in his little cowboy boots, his dark head bent with innocent obliviousness to anything other than the task at hand. Hannah's smile faded with the ever-present knowledge that Justin had yet to realize he had a father who didn't love him.

Unaware of her turmoil, Justin halted before her and announced, "I got hay for Jet. Can I give it to him?"

"Sure you can."

They walked over to the stall and Hannah opened the door just enough for Justin to dump the hay from the narrow wagon. The horse bent its head to the hay quietly enough, but Hannah sensed a restlessness in Jet's manner that she hadn't noticed before Devin had warned her about the horse—the glimmer of white showing at Jet's eyes, the quiver of energy in the muscles underlying his silky coat. Jet seemed larger than ever. Anxious to get the stall door closed once more, Hannah was relieved when Justin finished unloading his hay.

"I want to ride him."

Justin started inside and Hannah caught him by the arm, drawing him safely back. "Jet doesn't want to be ridden. Not right now."

"Yes, he does."

"No, he doesn't." Hannah slid the stall door shut. "He wants to play outside since I opened the door to his paddock. You've seen how he kicks and jumps. You don't want to ride him when he's doing that."

"Yes, I do." With much ceremony, Justin leaned over and spit.

"Justin Reese, that's the third time today I've seen you spit. That's bad manners."

"C.J. spits. He can spit real far." Justin's admiration was apparent.

She should have known. Hannah planted her hands on her hips.

"I don't care if C.J. can spit clear to Denver. You can't just walk around spitting all the time. That's the rule."

"Can I spit *sometimes?*"

Before Hannah could dash Justin's obvious hope, she caught sight of Devin silhouetted in the doorway against a backdrop of Colorado blue sky. She lowered her hands from her hips, conscious of her slightly swollen belly. Devin's pickup was parked outside, but he'd somehow caught her unawares, even though she'd expected him to show up sooner or later.

Devin pushed up his hat brim. "Men don't spit in front of ladies, Justin."

The impact of Devin's teasing gray eyes held Hannah speechless long enough for Justin to point out earnestly, "C.J. spits in front of Allie."

Standing beside his father, C.J. snorted. "Allie can spit as far as me."

Devin gave his son a quelling look, then told Justin, "Your mom was right. You can't go around spitting all the time. Now, out back of the barn, it's probably okay to spit. Wouldn't you say so, Hannah?"

If she didn't say so, Hannah thought, she'd be a wicked witch in Justin's eyes. She gritted her teeth. "That would be okay."

"C.J." Devin gave his son a nod.

With the brooding expression he seemed to reserve for mixed company, the boy walked past Hannah. She could tell by the way C.J. avoided her that he was still angry about seeing his father kiss her, not to mention the business with the horse. Bowing to Devin's wish, C.J. muttered to Justin, "Come on."

Justin abandoned his wagon to walk beside C.J. down the aisle toward the back of the barn, where the horses she boarded were kept pastured. Hannah almost groaned aloud when her son struggled to match his stride to C.J.'s, then tucked his hands in his back jeans pockets the same as C.J. did. They each had bucking horses on the back of their T-shirts. Hannah sincerely hoped there was nothing prophetic in that.

"You seem to be feeling better."

"Yes, I am. Thank you." Hannah left it at that and hoped Devin would, too. She'd rather he focus his attention on the fact that he was standing in what she'd heard described as a topnotch training center, even if Travis had seldom used it as such.

But his gaze remained on her, and Hannah resisted the urge to smooth back the tangles of her hair that had escaped her ponytail. With no makeup and her unruly curls drawn into a ponytail, she looked the way she always looked when working in the barn. It irritated her no end that she now wished she looked anything but.

Devin, of course, looked like some kind of cowboy fantasy, with his denim and boots accenting his dark good looks. His black hat was tipped just low enough to make it seem intimate to gaze into his eyes. So Hannah held his gaze deliberately and informed him, "I would have preferred to handle my son's lack of manners in my own way."

Tucking his hands into his front jeans pockets, Devin said patiently, "The boy's going to spit, Hannah. It's a given. The most you can do is teach him when and where to do it."

He was right of course. Hannah pursed her lips. "I'm sure C.J. will set him straight."

Devin only chuckled at that, stepping past her to look at Jet. To Hannah's chagrin, the horse raised his head to nuzzle Devin through the stall bars, giving a rumbling nicker that sounded like a warm greeting, as if he'd actually missed Devin.

Facing her once more, Devin pulled folded papers from the pocket of his shirt. "You'd better take a look at these. I've come to take the horse back to Sedalia."

He handed the papers to her and sauntered down the aisle with a confidence that irked Hannah. She unfolded the papers and gave them a cursory glance. It was simple to discern Jet's quarter horse pedigree, the triple *A*'s that confirmed the horse came from racing stock and—Hannah caught her lip—the lack of signature that would have proved a change in ownership.

Hannah slowly refolded the papers. Legally the horse was indeed still Devin's.

Hannah silently cursed Travis straight to hell.

With his penchant for buying horses, Travis would come through with Devin's money for Jet before he would child support. She *had* to get Devin to lease the barn, to keep Jet here until Travis paid for the horse.

Selling Jet was her best chance at getting the child support Travis owed, short of threatening her son's father with jail. Hannah couldn't bring herself to do that, mainly because she was afraid jail was exactly where Travis would end up.

When she caught up with him, Devin had stopped walking. He appeared to take note of the empty stalls, then gazed over the arena fence at the roping box and chutes at the end. Hannah felt a fleeting sense of guilt over taking advantage of C.J.'s divulgence of Devin's need for a place to train horses, but she assured herself the lease would be in C.J.'s best interests.

Reminded that Devin was determined to keep C.J. off the circuit, Hannah curled her hand confidently around the top rail of the fence and said with forced idleness, "Quite a place, isn't it? Travis intended to hold roping schools here. That's why he had the bunkhouse built and wanted a big arena and so many stalls."

"Intended to?"

"He never seemed to get past the planning stage. There was always another rodeo to go to."

"Hard to imagine owning all this and not putting it to use."

She'd often wondered herself how Travis had ignored all he had here at home, including herself and his child. Hannah tried to shrug her hurt and anger aside, but the bitterness crept into her voice. "Travis was never satisfied with anything he had."

"Travis Reese was a fool." Devin looked down at her then, and Hannah once again burned with a longing that had no place in her life just now. She was supposed to be planting the idea of a lease in Devin's mind, not the kind of thoughts that heated his gaze.

What was going through her mind? Devin wondered. Hannah's eyes were dark and filled with a mix of emotions he couldn't name. Meanwhile, his brevity of emotions came with an almost painful clarity. Desire for Hannah. And a sudden foolish urge to train his horses here in this arena.

C.J., he knew, would take exception to the idea. But Devin was desperate enough to find a place to lease and to keep his son off the circuit that he'd have danced with the devil to do so. In this case, the devil was pretty, kissable Hannah Reese.

Devin rested his arms on the fence and tried to ignore Hannah's small hand curled there, bare of her wedding ring. The barn, he rationalized, was available. Driving in, he'd seen that the horses she boarded were let out to pasture. The place was well ventilated for summer and sported heaters for the winter months. Weather would be a small factor in the training schedule here.

But a person didn't own a facility like this and let it sit empty unless they could afford the extravagance. Travis couldn't seem to pay for the horse he'd bought or pay his child support, but he'd apparently left Hannah sitting pretty after the divorce with both the ranch and the horse.

Recalling just then that said horse was *his,* Devin stepped away from the fence. He held out his hand for Jet's papers, feeling that misplaced twinge of guilt again when Hannah handed them over with obvious resentment. "I hope my taking the horse won't upset your son."

"He believes Jet belongs to his father. He doesn't expect the horse to stay."

Just as he'd learned not to expect his father to stay, Devin knew.

He could hear the boys outside the barn now, Justin's voice excited and full of hero worship, C.J.'s making him want to grin with its forced tolerance. He ought to go call his son inside, but Devin lingered, thoughts of work, of school for C.J., of Jolene's threat to take his son crowding his mind.

Hannah fidgeted beside him, likely anxious for him to leave. But damned if he could just walk out without asking about a lease. The worst she could say was no, and he'd be no worse off than he was already. So Devin asked, "Any chance you'd consider leasing the barn and bunkhouse to me?"

"I suppose I could consider it." Hannah gave a shrug, confirming Devin's theory that she was financially set. "But with that problem we have over the horse, getting along could prove difficult."

Devin pocketed the papers—*his* papers to *his* horse—and said pointedly, "I wouldn't have any problem getting along."

Hannah smiled sweetly. "I would. Unless, of course, you were willing to wait and deal with Travis about Jet."

In that moment Devin could have sworn Hannah knew just how badly he needed a place to train his horses. But even as his temper flared, he had to admire Hannah's tenacity where the horse—and her child's welfare—were concerned. His feelings for C.J. were as strong.

Still, she couldn't be serious. "You expect me to wait on Travis for money I'm not sure I'll get, while you keep the horse, meaning I can't sell it to someone else who might make an offer?"

"I guess if you look at it that way...yes, I do."

She *was* serious. If he wanted the lease, he would have to relinquish his claim on Jet until he caught up with Travis.

Devin wanted to wring Hannah's slender neck.

He wanted to kiss her.

He turned away before he gave in to either impulse, grabbing hold of the fence again and brooding about the matter.

Though it went against the grain, Devin figured that in agreeing all he'd be losing was time. He had his doubts Travis would come up with the money for the horse, figured he'd eventually have Jet back, anyway. In the meantime, he could keep an eye on Jet, maybe even work the horse back to its full potential, which he was sure Travis had let slip. Above all, he could keep C.J. off the circuit. Devin turned, his hands on his hips, and found Hannah waiting. "Let's see what kind of deal we can come up with."

In the end, Devin was left frowning over the fact that Hannah had gotten the better of him in a lease that would see C.J. through the upcoming school year. As they shook on the deal, he noted tersely, "You drive a hard bargain."

"I guess I have a knack for it," Hannah said hastily.

She had a little more color in her face today, Devin noted.

Her complexion had a dewy sheen from the exertion of working in the barn and chasing after a four-year-old boy. It made her look radiant, and the scent of her tempted him to the core. A proprietary feeling overcame the sense that he'd been gotten the better of, and Devin quickly released Hannah's hand.

He had enough problems without pursuing a woman in the face of his son's disapproval. At any rate, Devin thought wryly, Hannah had made it pretty clear when he'd kissed her that he'd better not try it again.

Looking down on her glossy hair, tempted to touch those silky curls, Devin realized what a trial it would be, living here, trying to keep his mind and his hands off her. He was almost glad when C.J. and Justin walked in to distract them, even knowing his son wouldn't take news of their move here gracefully.

Aware getting straight to the point worked best with his son, Devin said, "C.J., we've got horses to haul."

"That mean we're taking Jet home?"

"I'll be dealing with Travis about that later. I've made plans to lease this barn, so we'll be hauling stock here from Sedalia."

C.J. didn't disappoint him, but Devin was surprised when the boy aimed his accusing look Hannah's way. "I never should have told you about the lease being over."

Jamming his hat down low, C.J. stomped past them up the aisle. Hannah reached for Justin to keep him from following, but he was too quick, and Devin's hard gaze stayed her as effectively as an iron grip.

"You knew my lease was up."

Hannah recognized that tone. She licked her dry lips. "C.J. mentioned you needed a place."

There was fire in Devin's smoky eyes. She would not be intimidated, would not feel guilty. Knowledge of his need may have given her some advantage, but Devin had the edge of knowing the business better than she did. "This was as much your deal as mine," she reminded him. "You made an offer and I accepted. I didn't force you to shake my hand."

Hannah was certain it was only the reminder of the handshake that had Devin giving a curt nod of acknowledgment. But his eyes were still dark enough to have her wary of what his parting words might be.

Devin caught her by surprise, raising his hand, gently twining a stray curl at her cheek around his finger. "Looks like I'm going to have to watch my step with you in more ways than one, Hannah Reese."

Chapter Four

"I can take care of Jet myself."

Aware Devin could peel the pitchfork from her grasp anytime if he chose, Hannah clung to it as tenaciously as she clung to her deceptions. Though she and Devin had come to terms on a lease, she felt a keen reluctance to reveal to him either her inexperience with horses or her pregnancy.

Sweat dampened the underarm seam of her sleeveless white shirt, the unsnapped waist of her jeans beneath her shirttails digging into her ever-swelling belly. Hannah determinedly swallowed the taste of morning sickness. She wanted nothing more than to hand over the chore of cleaning Jet's stall. But now that Devin had ordered her to do so, she'd be damned if she would.

"I reckon we should have ironed out the details of this agreement a little better." Devin stood with his hands on his hips, his weight shifted to one booted foot. His eyes were smoky coals below his hat brim. "You said yourself you didn't have time for the horse with your boy to take care of. And that horse needs more than just being turned out in a paddock to play."

Hannah narrowed her gaze right back at him. Having arrived only two days ago, Devin probably had yet to hang up his spurs. But he was already trying to take over with Jet, despite the deal they'd made.

Still, there was a grain of sense to what Devin said. The horse was only worth the extent of its training. If Travis showed up, it would be to her benefit to have Jet at his prime, considering she was likely to wind up with the horse to sell rather than the money for child support.

Hannah was prepared to compromise, to tell Devin he could work the horse and she would see to its care, when the crunch of gravel and hum of an engine outside caught her attention. Keeping hold of the pitchfork, Hannah went to the door, shielding her eyes from the bright midmorning sun as she looked for Justin. He and C.J. appeared from beside the barn, C.J.'s step faltering at the sight of Allie climbing out of the sporty white Jeep, along with her mother.

Hannah smiled a little wistfully. Wearing a pressed flowered shirt with crisp blue jeans, Tilly looked as neat and fresh as she, Hannah, was unkempt and worn. The sun that highlighted Tilly's bright tresses seemed to bake right through to Hannah's brain. Then she realized much of the heat came from Devin,

standing at her shoulder. The short sleeves of his
faded red shirt brushed her bare shoulder, and his hip
nudged hers. When her stomach fluttered, Hannah assured herself it was nothing five months wouldn't
cure. With a warning look at Devin, she leaned the
pitchfork against the wall and went to greet her friend,
only to have Devin follow.

While Tilly had come on the pretext of delivering
homemade cookies, Hannah quickly realized her
good-natured friend only wanted to make sure fences
were mended between Allie and C.J. now that Devin
had moved onto the ranch. Hannah appreciated the
gesture. It was good for Justin to see that the two
twelve-year-olds had made up after their argument,
although Justin still didn't understand why Allie
hadn't liked C.J.'s kiss when Allie always liked *his*
kisses.

They stood eating cookies and talking, C.J. and Allie endearingly awkward, Hannah grateful her nose
and stomach were amenable to Tilly's treat. When the
telephone rang in the barn, Tilly shooed Hannah off,
saying she had to get back to work. Hannah admon-
ished Justin, his hands full of cookie, to steer clear of
the Jeep when Tilly drove out. Then she hurried to
answer the telephone.

Minutes later, after confirming with a neighboring
farmer that she wanted delivery of an extra load of
hay this month, Hannah hung up the receiver and
peered out the barn door. She'd half expected Devin
to come in and take over with Jet while she was on
the phone. But while Tilly had bid her adieu minutes

ago, her friend was still talking with Devin, even though Allie had gotten into the Jeep and the boys were now ambling toward the barn. Hannah frowned; she knew she shouldn't be feeling jealous. So why was she?

"Is Allie still mad?" Justin's voice came breathlessly as he trotted to keep pace with C.J.'s stride, his little boots kicking up small dust whirls. Distracted, Hannah suspected Justin was concerned because Allie hadn't wanted to play, trying to act grown-up in C.J.'s presence. Despite C.J.'s stolen kiss, Allie apparently liked him. One corner of Hannah's mouth curved wryly. The Bartlett men seemed to have that effect on women.

C.J. shrugged in response to Justin's question. "Who knows with women."

Hannah caught her lip over that as the boys neared the barn. C.J. was still irked with her for leasing his father the barn, in addition to her kissing his father and claiming she owned Jet. He wouldn't appreciate her amusement.

"I want to go spit." Justin spoke with every confidence that C.J. would want to go spit, too.

"I got to practice my roping. I can't just ride broncs if I want to win an all-round championship." C.J. veered toward the bunkhouse, probably for his coveted rope.

"Okay." Justin trailed after him, apparently unaware he'd been dismissed. Hannah's heart squeezed for her son. She considered intervening, calling Justin back to her side before C.J. could send him away. But

C.J. simply ignored Justin, and Hannah's attention was eventually drawn by Devin's low-pitched chuckle.

He'd rested his hand on the hood of Tilly's Jeep and now pushed back his hat brim, letting the sun burn down on his already bronzed face. His white teeth flashed with his wide smile, and whatever he said had Tilly shaking back her sleek hair and laughing. Hannah felt her stomach clench and knew it had nothing to do with the baby she carried and everything to do with the attention Devin was paying her pretty, available friend.

After a moment she frowned. Devin and Tilly seemed engrossed in their conversation. Then Devin suddenly looked her way and Hannah drew back with a grimace. She didn't want Devin to think she was spying on him. She was glad he was flirting around, just as she was glad he intended to "watch his step" with her.

Still, their drifting laughter made her feel agitated. She grasped the pitchfork from where she'd leaned it against the barn wall and sent it clattering into the bed of the wheelbarrow. Scooping loosened curls toward the black band that held her hair in a ponytail, Hannah pushed the wheelbarrow along the aisle to Jet's stall. She ought to have better sense than to let herself be stirred by another cowboy.

As for Tilly, Hannah hoped her friend would be careful. Devin's flirtations were apparently superficial, and despite C.J.'s intervention, probably too numerous to count on one hand.

Hannah interrupted her mental tirade to set aside the wheelbarrow and slide open the door to Jet's stall. She stepped inside, certain by the way the horse pricked its ears, its muscles tensing, that it sensed her nervousness. Jet was well mannered enough that she could get the paddock door at the back of the stall open, but sometimes in his eagerness to get outside, the horse rushed by before she was completely out of the way. And there was more of herself to get out of the way every day now, Hannah thought ruefully, placing her hand protectively over her belly.

"Easy, Jet." Hannah kept one eye on the horse as she slid the door shut and sidled toward the back of the stall. Jet inched closer, giving an impatient snort. With great effort Hannah stood her ground, trying to push aside the heavy bolt and open the paddock door.

But the bolt wouldn't budge, and her heart beat faster as Jet pawed the floor, his shod hoof flashing, sending straw flying. Hannah jerked at the bolt in frustration, fighting stereotyped images of rearing stallions with flailing hooves, compliments of reruns of TV Westerns. Jet gave another commanding snort just as she managed to slip the bolt free.

Hannah breathed a sigh of relief. She thought she heard Devin say her name from the aisle, but she didn't dare take her eyes off Jet now, aware the horse had spied daylight and was ready to bolt. As was her custom, Hannah gave the door a hard shove to enable Jet to pass through cleanly.

Jet lunged toward the opening. But Hannah hadn't quite backed clear and the horse jostled her in passing. She lost her balance and staggered back with a cry, reaching behind her to break her fall.

The opening slam of the stall door reached her ears through her dismay. Devin caught her beneath the arms, tumbling back with her to the straw-covered floor of the stall. Hannah's breath whooshed from her lungs with the impact. Sprawled on her back atop him, she blinked to see past the haze of dust motes swirling in the air above them.

Devin's body was lean and hard. But it accommodated her curves perfectly, her head settling against the crook of his shoulder, his hips forming a cradle that she nestled in securely. Too securely. Aware that his hands rested dangerously near her breasts and that her belly was showing its shape to her disadvantage, Hannah attempted to unwind her legs from his.

Devin tightened his grip beneath Hannah's arms, aware of the soft mounds of her breasts just below his hands. He let out an exasperated breath. She'd scared the life out of him, or at least ten years' worth of it.

He'd gone along with her charade of being a horse-woman—he hadn't a clue why she seemed to think it was necessary—but looking down at the disarray of her black curls across his shoulder, at the disheveled state of her clothes over slender bones that could easily have been broken, he saw red. In one swift move that sent his hat toppling, he had her on her back in the straw. He loomed over her, pleased with the wariness in her eyes.

But somehow his reprimand got lost with one blink of her curling lashes. All he could think was how creamy Hannah's skin looked framed by wisps of dark silky curls. Her breasts rose and fell rapidly now beneath her white shirt, and drawn to those soft curves, Devin lowered his body to hers for the barest of touches. Sliding his hand beneath her to cup the back of her head, he leaned in and kissed her.

Her lips were incredibly soft, deliciously moist. With the surprised hitch of her breath, Devin took advantage and kissed her more deeply, until he felt the subtle give of her body as she relented and kissed him back. He wanted to touch her now, really touch her. But despite her apparent surrender to the kiss, she tensed. So Devin poured his frustration into kissing her, contenting himself to steal his hand across Hannah's belly—

He stilled his palm over the soft swell he found, let his lips hover on Hannah's. She was carrying a child.

Surprise and concern edged past his passion. He opened his eyes and looked down at Hannah's flushed face. Her eyes were closed, her breathing shallow. After a moment she turned her cheek, her soft hair fluttering over his arm as gently as the life that stirred within her. Devin pressed his palm more securely against Hannah's belly, awed. "The baby is moving."

Devin thought of the baby his son had once been, marveling over the wonder of woman even as he worried about Hannah's well-being. Relief coursed

through him when she turned her face to him and
opened her eyes.

"I think it's a girl this time..." she murmured.

The hesitance in her voice revealed an uncertainty
Devin had earlier glimpsed in Hannah. In addition to
trying to raise her son and run this ranch alone, Devin
figured he now knew the full extent of Hannah's need
to find Travis. And he finally understood those times
she'd appeared ill, the excuses she'd made. Aloud
he wondered, "Does anyone else know about this
baby?"

Hannah sighed. "Just myself, my obstetrician and
now you. Let me up, please."

Devin leaned back, pulling Hannah to a sitting position. Golden stems of straw clung to her tangled
ponytail and spilled off her shirt. "Are you sure you
aren't hurt?"

"I'm fine."

Devin wasn't sure "fine" applied to a woman in
her situation, but he knew better than to say so. He
plucked stems of straw from her hair, relieved by the
spark that came back to her eyes. She batted his hand
aside, gave her hair a shake that had curls swinging
and straw raining back over her shirt. When she
caught him eyeing her shrewdly, she said, "The baby
is Travis's, if that's what you're wondering."

"I figured that much." Devin propped his elbow
on his raised knee, suddenly inclined to know more.
"Think knowing so will bring Travis back home?"
Back to your bed...

"I didn't get pregnant intentionally, trying to trick Travis into staying," Hannah said with indignation.

"I never thought you did."

Hannah settled back a little. Then she lowered her head, resting her hand over her stomach with infinite care. "I kept hoping we could work things out. I was wrong."

Hannah's sigh touched him. It was obvious that she'd done all she could to save her marriage. And he could see that she wanted this baby. He better understood her reluctance to get involved with another man, knew her defenses would only be stronger where he was concerned now that he'd discovered her pregnancy. Knowledge of the baby should have made him feel more guarded, too, but it only seemed to intensify the solicitous feelings he had for Hannah.

"Justin came really fast when he was born. He was big and…" Hannah looked up then, almost shyly. "It gets pretty technical, but what it amounts to is the doctor told me there was so much damage, another conception would be impossible. I might have been foolish enough to think sex might change Travis's mind just before the divorce was finalized, but I never thought I'd have another child. But, since I did get pregnant, I should be able to carry my baby safely and deliver by cesarean section."

"Miracles happen."

"Most wouldn't judge so, all things considered."

"I always wanted more kids." It felt right to Devin, somehow, telling Hannah, and for the moment it eased the bitterness he felt toward Jolene. "Jolene didn't want the son we had. She's had a change of heart lately, but only because she's hurting for money and sees a chance to collect child support."

Hannah stiffened at the mention of child support, and he knew her thoughts were on Travis as she said tersely, "I guess we're each living a different facet of the same story."

"I don't suppose Travis will be forthcoming with support for this baby?"

Hannah averted her gaze, smoothing her hand over her belly. "Once I was sure I was pregnant, I let myself hope another baby would draw Travis home. But seeing how he's put Justin behind him, I suspect the news will send him running to his lawyer, trying to get out of paying."

"I guess even if you don't need the money, you want it for your children," Devin said musingly. "This place has to be worth a pretty penny."

Hannah's ensuing silence was telling. "Mortgaged?"

She raised her chin. "I intend to make it mine and my children's."

Devin was getting a clearer picture all the time, and it wasn't pretty. Raking his fingers through his hair, he shoved on his hat. Then, propelled by the anger that pulsed through him, he pushed to his feet and reached to grasp Hannah's hands, hauling her up. Even pregnant, she was featherlight and Devin felt a surge of protectiveness he knew Hannah wouldn't appreciate. Still, as he let go of her he advised, "You need to force Travis's hand, Hannah. Take him to court for the money.''

"No." Her reply was instantaneous. "I can't do that. I *won't* do that.''

Her reluctance to make Travis face up to his responsibility irritated Devin no end. "Why the hell not? It would be for the sake of your kids—kids Travis conceived." The very thought rankled.

"My children are the exact reason why I'm not taking Travis to court. I can't bear the thought of Justin someday finding out I was responsible for sending his father to jail. Surely you can understand that.''

"Justin just might be grateful when the money you get from Travis puts him through college," Devin said bitingly.

"Either way, it's my decision to make.''

Hannah dusted off the seat of her jeans, and Devin knew he'd been put in his place, which was no place in her life. But she needed someone to turn to, and he told her, "You should tell your family and friends about this, Hannah, instead of trying to stand alone.''

"I know that." Hannah raised her arms ballerina-like, tightening the band on her ponytail. Then she lowered her hands to straighten her shirt. "I just thought Travis should be the first to know.''

That didn't sit well, either, and Devin knew why, just as he knew this proprietary feeling he kept having for Hannah wasn't in the best interests of his son. Or himself.

But when Hannah walked out of the stall and grabbed the pitchfork, Devin followed her. It had been bad enough worrying about her around Jet when he knew she'd lied about being experienced with horses. The fact that he knew she was pregnant increased that worry tenfold.

"Don't even think about it." Devin grasped the pitchfork. The instant his hand came to rest against hers, Hannah released her hold, stepping back. No fool, Devin read the sign clearly. She felt the fire that sparked between them the same as he, but it was plain she had no intention of getting involved with another cowboy. Knowing that was for the best, Devin turned away to roll the wheelbarrow into the stall.

When the chore was done, he wasn't surprised to come back in the barn to find Hannah spreading the bale of fresh straw he'd tossed in the stall. She said nothing, only cast him a glance that was both wary and warning. Just the sight of her standing in that fresh bed of straw had his hormones flaming.

"I'll go check on those boys," Devin told her.

"Thanks." Her words came on a sigh, and he knew she was grateful he hadn't pushed. She needed that bit of independence the chore gave her to shore up her confidence. But while he could understand Hannah's need to stand on her own, Devin figured she better get used to having him around, backing her up, for the duration of his lease.

He strode away, and, finished with the stall, Hannah stepped into the aisle to lean heavily against the pitchfork, watching him go. The boys waylaid him outside the barn with demands to lasso fence posts with them. Hannah smiled wryly at her son's sudden passion for roping and dislike of baseball. For whatever reason, Justin admired C.J. to the extent that his loyalty to his beloved Allie was put to the test.

But as Devin ruffled Justin's hair, Hannah felt a prickling of fear for her son. Justin had fast overcome his shyness with Devin, lighting up around him as if every minute in Devin's presence was the Fourth of July.

And she wasn't much better, Hannah thought ruefully, thinking of how she'd let Devin kiss her, of the way she'd kissed him back. He had a way of reaching past her defenses, of making her yearn for things she'd learned better than to expect. But even knowing so, she couldn't pull her gaze from Devin, from the picture he made with their boys as they copied his long-legged stride, his shadow stretching past theirs like a promise of what would someday be.

She caught herself as she realized what that promise meant. Devin was a rodeo cowboy, the same as Travis. He'd only left the circuit for the sake of his son, and not long ago. That didn't mean he'd left forever. The temptation to lean on him might be strong, but she couldn't let the sense of security that came with having him around lull her into depending on him in any way.

Still, Hannah watched until Devin walked out of sight.

Chapter Five

Devin hefted his saddle onto the rack in the tack compartment of his four-horse trailer, sweat gathering beneath his hatband. The day was going to be a hot one, the sun burning his back through his white shirt though it was only seven in the morning. C.J. was giving the horses in the pasture their supplemental feed, something Hannah would take exception to, but he wasn't about to leave for the rodeo in Cheyenne, worrying about Hannah and Justin out in the heat near the stock.

Without Jet to take care of, Hannah didn't spend much time at the barn, a fact that both relieved and tormented Devin. He liked knowing she wasn't handling Jet on her own, but he was so intent on watching for her when she wasn't around that he'd almost gotten himself unseated by a colt he was training. That had caused his son to look at him long and hard.

Thinking of C.J. brought to mind his reluctance to go to Cheyenne. Jolene's betrayals didn't stop his son from wanting to see his mother, and Jolene had promised C.J. she'd be at Cheyenne, where she'd always placed well in the barrel racing. Devin was sorely tempted to skip the rodeo.

But he'd paid his entry fees and he had a chance to make a profitable sale on the roping horse he had ready; a lot of top hands made Cheyenne. Remembering this, Devin resolutely slammed shut the compartment door, ready now to load his horse. Even if this rodeo meant an encounter with Jolene, it would do him good to spend the upcoming days at Cheyenne, to put Hannah Reese behind him, at least until he returned each night.

But Devin didn't take another step; he was transfixed by the sight of Hannah walking from the house with her son, the soft morning light shimmering on their black curls. He thought again that Travis Reese was a fool, felt a tug at his heart as Justin went running toward the barn where his father should have been, but wasn't.

Hannah raised her slender arms to tuck back strands of hair that had come loose from a gold clasp. She was nearly five months pregnant, but a man would hardly notice with her pale denim shirt worn loose over her new jeans, the ones she'd brought home in a pink-and-blue-striped sack from a maternity shop in Greeley.

But now that he knew, Devin recognized the signs and wondered how he'd missed the way the breeze fleetingly molded her shirt to the shape of her belly, the way she would place her hand protectively over her unborn child. He'd definitely come to recognize that "about to be sick" look that washed all the color from her cheeks. She was wearing it now, and Devin suffered a man's helpless concern.

But as she drew near, he noted how her boots scuffed the gravel, how her voice carried a determined note as she warned Justin not to go near the horses. Justin veered past him with a grin, heading for the barn to find C.J. while Hannah aimed her stride his way. Despite her pale cheeks, there were the telltale sparks in her eyes he'd come to recognize. Though he could easily guess why, as she stopped before him, Devin only said innocently, "Morning, Hannah."

She chose to ignore his greeting, glaring up at him, instead. "I thought you had a rodeo to go to."

"We're just about ready to leave."

"So why have you got C.J. doing *my* chores?"

Slow heat built within Devin, in part from the challenge she issued, but mostly from the tempting picture she made, her boots toe-to-toe with his, her usual reserve forgotten in her fit of temper. "Because I've got enough to worry about today without picturing you here being trampled while your boy watches on."

"I'm perfectly capable of feeding the stock, whether you're here or not."

"I didn't mean to imply you weren't," Devin said carefully. Hannah had yet to come clean about her lack of experience as a horsewoman. But she *was* capable of feeding the stock, so he told her, "I was just thinking of the baby, and I wanted the peace of mind of knowing you weren't out in this heat. I've turned my stock out to graze for the day, and I'll take care of them when I get back.''

Surprise flickered in her eyes, as if it was a novelty to have someone looking out for her. Devin bit back an oath aimed at Travis.

"I guess...I should thank you," Hannah said haltingly, and he knew she wouldn't care for how vulnerable she seemed with that admission. Deciding to press the advantage, Devin repeated an offer he'd made earlier in the week. "Are you sure you don't want me to give Travis a message if I see him in Cheyenne?"

Hannah squared her shoulders. "I'm sure. I'd appreciate if you'd let me know if Travis is there, but I'll wait until the final day of the rodeo to talk to him about the baby and the child support."

"I could talk to him for you, Hannah." Devin curled his hands, surprised by how much he relished the opportunity.

"Thanks, but no. That's something I have to do myself."

He could sense her drawing away again, just as she had after he'd kissed her. Though he knew it was for the best, frustration had him feeling roped and tied. He sighed. "I want you to know I won't pressure Travis about my money for Jet."

"I'm not asking that of you." Hannah raised her chin and reminded him, "If Travis pays you, I'll get my money one way or another."

He didn't like the idea of Hannah standing up to Travis, trying to claim the horse, and he grumbled, "It would be a lot easier if Travis would just pay the child support."

But Travis wasn't in the habit of making things easy for her, and it pricked at Hannah's pride to see that awareness in Devin's eyes. That same pride enabled her to push aside all temptation to lean on Devin's broad shoulders, no mean feat considering those shoulders were handsomely clad in a white tailored pearl-snapped shirt.

C.J. emerged from the barn then, leading a bay horse, Justin sitting astride, beaming.

"Daylight's burning," C.J. called to his father. And before Hannah could work up a worry over Justin riding the horse, C.J. unceremoniously hauled her son down and out of the way and proceeded to load the horse like a practiced hand.

"Don't let the boy ride beneath the barn door," Devin reprimanded C.J. But Hannah suspected it was C.J.'s impatience to leave that had Devin grimacing, and she murmured, "I guess C.J.'s hoping to see his mother at the rodeo."

Devin moved closer, so that the sun cast his shadow upon her. "She promised to be there," he confided, adding tersely, "If I didn't have this horse ready to sell, I wouldn't go. Jolene's let the boy down time and again, but he can't see it."

Hannah suspected all C.J. saw was his father and mother getting together again.

C.J. came around to tie off the horse at the front

of the trailer. His eyes flashed at the sight of his father standing so close to her. On impulse Hannah told him, "Thank you for doing those chores, C.J. I'd be willing to pay you to take them over for me." Her days of hefting hay bales were pretty much over.

C.J.'s mix of surprise and suspicion should have been insulting, but knowing from where his wariness stemmed, Hannah couldn't take offense, even when he said, "Long as I'm stuck here until the lease is over, I reckon I might as well take the job."

"C.J.—" Devin spoke sharply to his son, but Hannah raised her hand in a staying gesture, encouraged by C.J.'s acceptance of sorts.

"C.J. has a right to be angry with me." Hannah faced the boy squarely. "I regret taking advantage after you confided in me. Maybe, if I add homemade cookies to the deal, you'll accept my apology, as well as the offer."

C.J. thought it over for so long Hannah started to feel she was the recipient of more mistrust than she was due, leading her to think C.J. wasn't as unaware of his mother's shortcomings as Devin believed. His T-shirt for the day, featuring bull riding and labeled "No Bull," combined with that calculating look in his eye to confirm her belief that little got past C.J. Bartlett. Confident he would recognize the sincerity of her offer, Hannah wasn't surprised when C.J. finally said, "It's a deal."

Hannah held out her hand to the boy. He reached out reluctantly for a handshake before turning and climbing into the truck.

"He's not as easily charmed as I am," came Devin's low-pitched voice near her ear.

Hannah's smile faltered, a subtle shiver making its way down her spine.

"That was a nice gesture," he added more seriously. "C.J. will appreciate it someday, if he doesn't now."

"I hope so." Hannah's reluctance to see Devin leave sifted through her need for him do so. But the sight of her son standing by, a forlorn little cowboy, reminded her the separation was for the best. "You'd better be going. Daylight's burning, remember?"

Devin chuckled. He strode over to Justin and crouched before him, exchanging a word that put a smile back on her son's face. Justin ran to her side and Devin walked around to climb into the truck. As he drove down the lane, his white-and-silver rig took on a pearllike glow in the hazy morning sun. When he turned onto the blacktop stretching toward the purple rise of the Rockies, Hannah thought how the sun would be bedding down behind the mountains by the time he came home....

"Devin's going to bring me Indian feathers from the rodeo," Justin announced, interrupting images Hannah knew better than to dwell on.

"That's nice of him." Hannah made herself smile, knowing she needed to discourage Devin's gift giving, aware it would only contribute to her son's heartbreak once Devin was gone. She thought again that it was for the best that Devin would be spending the coming days at Cheyenne. But knowing that didn't seem to keep her from anticipating the nights, when he would return.

Justin curled his arms about her leg, leaning his slight weight against her. And while the urge was strong to stand here with him and watch until Devin's rig was completely out of sight, Hannah resolutely turned herself and her son toward the house.

But it was hard to put Devin out of her mind with Justin reminding her of his existence the whole day long. Trying unsuccessfully to interest Justin in crayons and colored paper, Hannah realized her efforts to keep him out of the barn and away from Devin and C.J. hadn't kept him from cherishing every moment in their presence. Justin seemed to pick up on her desire to put the Bartletts behind them for a while, and he had just enough of her stubbornness to make the day a trying one in his persistence to foil her efforts.

But Justin's willfulness proved his undoing in the end. That night, stubborn even in sleep, he lay at the end of his bed by the open window, having lost the battle to await Devin's return. Hannah sighed as she covered him with just a sheet. She hoped now that Devin remembered the Indian feather. It was bad enough her son hadn't known what fatherly love felt like. She didn't want him to be disappointed by the first man who actually gave him some attention.

Hannah walked down the hall and went out on the porch as she had so many times before when Travis had gone to the rodeo. She could sit at the east end and look over the dark sweep of prairie, broken only by a stand of cottonwoods along a shallow creek bed, or sit at the west end and view the cool shadows of the far-off mountains. Now she sat in the middle on a white wicker chair, watching down the starlit lane with no expectations.

This morning she'd spent time figuring the bank balance, which wasn't quite so discouraging since Devin's arrival, but would have looked better with four months of child support added in. Afterward she'd raked and swept in the barn, which seemed emptier than ever with Devin gone and his horses turned out. It was a good reminder that she would eventually have to arrange another lease, for Devin would likely buy a place of his own or resolve his problems with Jolene and get back on the rodeo circuit.

A temperate westerly breeze eased the day's heat from her skin. Right now Devin was probably celebrating or simply enjoying time away from the ranch. Hannah rested her head against the high back of the chair and closed her eyes in an effort to relax, but that only sharpened the image of Devin holding some cowgirl in his arms. There was a country band featured after the rodeo tonight, and she knew Devin liked to hold a woman when he danced....

Opening her eyes, Hannah pushed to her feet, the wicker chair crackling in her wake. She was fretting over Devin the same as she'd once fretted over Travis. How smart was that? If anything, she ought to be worrying about whether or not Travis was in Cheyenne. Patting her stomach as much to comfort herself as the baby she carried, Hannah went into the house to shower and go to bed.

She was knotting the sash on the pale blue cotton wrapper that went over her new oversize pajamas and contemplating a glass of milk when she heard wheels rolling over gravel. The sound was heavy in night air gone still. Every tense muscle in her body relaxed, a telling reaction, which should have sparked more worry. Hannah only turned out the light and went to the bedroom window. The sound of truck doors opening and closing echoed as she pushed aside the heavy curtain to peer through the lace panel.

Devin had apparently left his horse trailer in Cheyenne. His white shirt flashed like a beacon in the nebulous mix of pale moonlight and the single security lamp near the barn. C.J. came to stand beside him and Devin spoke to him, his voice hushed so that only his compassionate tone, not the words, reached her. When he rested his hand on C.J.'s shoulder and C.J. bowed his head, Hannah turned from the window, feeling as if she was invading their privacy.

Sounds of him and C.J. bringing their stock into the barn reached through the screen as she left the room, her bare feet quiet on the hardwood floor. She pushed her fingers through the wet ringlets of her hair, walking down the dimly lit hall, past the darkened living room to the kitchen, concern enfolding her with every step. Devin's sympathy for his son had been easily discernible, and it wasn't hard to guess that somehow Jolene had disappointed C.J. at the rodeo.

Hannah was rinsing her empty milk glass when a

light knock on the side porch door rattled the panes and made her heart leap. Instinctively she pulled the sash of her wrapper tighter, then rolled her eyes at the result and loosened it over her round belly. She crossed to the door and opened it to find Devin leaning there, dusty and worn, his hat pushed back on his head, his gray eyes tired and full of a pain she recognized and felt clear to her core.

"Come in." Hannah pulled the door wider.

Devin declined with a glance at the bunkhouse, which sat in clear view of the west side of the house. "I'd better not."

But he moved aside, subtly inviting her to come out. Hannah slipped past him, conscious of her blue pajama bottoms pooling over the top of her bare feet. With her wrapper crossed securely over her breasts, she was hardly a picture of seduction, but that didn't keep her from being seduced herself by the sight of a handsome cowboy in the moonlight.

"I got these for Justin." Devin ran feathers through his curled hand, soft brown ones with black tips, held together by copper beads and rawhide.

Hannah smiled and accepted them, unconsciously running them across her palm the way Devin had run them across his. "He'll love them. He was waiting for you—"

Hannah broke off, embarrassed. She didn't want to sound as if Devin owed them an explanation whenever he got back late. "I mean Justin was anxious, knowing you'd mentioned Indian feathers."

She chanced a glance up and read the question in

Devin's eyes all too clearly. Had she been waiting for him, too? Hannah feared the answer glowed plainly in her eyes.

"I thought you'd sleep easier knowing Travis was at the rodeo. He took fourth in the calf roping and bronc riding."

Hannah felt something of Devin's tiredness come over her then. How much easier it would be if she didn't need any support from Travis. But she did, and Hannah resigned herself to that fact for now. "Thanks for telling me. I'll make sure to see Travis next weekend."

Devin's displeasure about that was obvious, the grim line of his mouth enhanced by the blue-black shadow of his beard. But he didn't offer to speak with Travis on her behalf again, and Hannah was grateful. She wasn't up to sparring with Devin, not with the stars shining down and her so aware of his strong shoulders to lean on. He shifted as if stiff and sore, and Hannah asked, "How did your roping horse do today?"

"Beat Travis out of third and caught the eye of a California cowboy." Devin rolled his shoulder and winced, but a glint came into his eyes. "I finished third in the bronc riding, too."

Was that a hint of satisfaction she heard in Devin's voice at having bested Travis in both events? Hannah couldn't be sure, but she knew she shouldn't enjoy the fact that he'd done so, considering she needed Travis to win the child support he owed her. Striving to sound impartial, she said, "Sounds like you had a good day."

The light faded from Devin's eyes and he turned his gaze briefly toward the bunkhouse, ablaze now with lights. "Jolene was there. We hung around so C.J. could watch the barrel races. He was hoping she'd ask him to stay on with her for the rodeo, but she knocked down a barrel and wasn't in the best of moods. Plus she's already got a traveling companion this trip. Bull rider up from Texas."

Devin's disgust was obvious. Hannah thought of C.J., recalling his downcast face. She couldn't imagine herself not wanting to spend time with Justin, couldn't imagine hurting him that way. All she could think of to say was, "I'm sorry, Devin."

"Thanks."

Devin's gaze was intense, lingering on her lips before flickering to her bare feet and back. Hannah curled her toes against the thrill that swept through her. She knew better, and so did he…

Devin pulled a flat white box from his back pocket. "I got something for you, too. It's called a 'dream catcher.' Native Americans believe if you hang one in your lodge, all bad dreams will perish and only good dreams will find their way through."

Hannah tucked Justin's feathers in her wrapper pocket, then took the box, her hands trembling slightly. Travis had never brought home a gift from the rodeo for her. She probably shouldn't accept this from Devin.

But a soft sigh escaped as she opened the box and

lifted out an intricate web of white and turquoise feathers.

"I figured you could use some good dreams," Devin said, and Hannah realized how starved for affection she must be for his kind words to touch her so.

"This is beautiful."

"So are you, Hannah Reese." Devin's husky voice stilled her, even as it brought every nerve in her being to aching attention. She couldn't bring herself to look at him, and she leaned weakly against the porch rail, thinking the dream catcher must be working now. Travis had stopped telling her she was pretty a long time ago...

Because she'd been pregnant, as she was now. Hannah sighed as reality swept over her. "Thank you, but you don't have to say that. I've been pregnant before and my ego can handle it."

"The baby adds...luster." Devin cupped her chin, gently raising her downcast face, and Hannah caught her breath with the warm caress of his callused fingers. As he slipped his other hand around her shoulders, she closed her eyes and held her dream catcher close to her heart.

"It's like magic, isn't it?" Devin whispered.

And it was. She could all but hear the stars shine as he held her. Still she told him, "I don't believe in magic anymore."

"I don't put much stock in it myself," Devin murmured. Then he kissed her, anyway, his mouth warm and firm and magical on hers.

When he left her, Hannah didn't open her eyes, just

listened to the quiet scuff of his boots along the porch and down the steps. The sound grew muffled as he crossed the yard, then the sharp crunch of gravel told her he was near the bunkhouse. She finally did look, but Devin had gone inside. Hannah gazed a long while at the brightly lit windows and closed door, then she went into the house, closing her door, as well.

So the days of the rodeo went, hot and dusty and long until night, when Devin came to her porch to tell her how Travis had done. A sense of caution prevailed now, Devin bringing her no more gifts and Hannah making sure she had on her boots when he arrived. Still, she found irrational satisfaction in the fact that Devin had thus far outridden and outroped her ex-husband. And Justin was more excited about the chance to watch Devin bronc-ride than he was at the prospect of watching his father. Hannah despaired over that. But she wasn't going to speak up on Travis's behalf. She was through building up expectations that Travis was not likely to fulfill.

Chapter Six

The final day of the rodeo arrived. Hannah didn't look forward to confronting Travis about child support or to revealing her pregnancy. His reaction would likely be as blistering as the weather. But for Justin's sake and the baby's, she was determined to talk to him.

Hannah scooped her hair into a clasp of pearls, then lowered her hands to her sides, gazing into the dresser mirror. Her denim dress still adequately hid her pregnancy. She didn't want Travis noticing her condition from a distance; he'd disappear before she could say "child support."

A wave of nausea swept over her then, and Hannah pressed her hand to her lips. Her sickness would be harder to hide than her belly. Fortunately her sense of smell had returned to normal and her morning sickness had finally confined itself to mornings.

She pulled on her boots and grabbed her small black purse and keys. Justin had dressed himself at dawn in his new black cowboy hat and boots and was already outside. Before heading to the barn, she hurried to collect the cookies she'd baked to go along with C.J.'s first week's salary. She hoped Devin wouldn't mind her following them to Cheyenne. If her truck had a flat tire or engine problems, it would be nice to have help, considering her condition. As for the trip home, if it worked out that they left together, fine. If not, she would manage. She didn't expect Devin to change his plans for her.

As she neared the barn, Hannah could hear the boys out back, Justin no doubt hampering C.J. in his efforts to feed the stock. Devin was turning his horses out to graze again, and she went over to the white pole fence to watch. The horses milled restlessly at first, Devin moving among them, which worried her but seemed to have a calming effect on the horses. She could hear him talking to them. A brown colt she recognized as one that had bucked and almost thrown Devin one day trailed after him as he walked over.

Her heart responded to Devin's lazy graceful cowboy gait with a hard yearning beat. She seemed destined to be attracted to a cowboy—this cowboy—no matter that common sense deemed it foolish.

He was wearing that wicked black shirt again, Hannah noted, the one he'd worn the first time he'd kissed her. Her truck keys dug into her palm as she gripped them. When he was but a few steps away, she braced herself with an indrawn breath, affected as always by the sight of his handsome clean-shaven face.

"I have C.J.'s salary and cookies," she said. "And, if you don't mind, I thought I'd follow you to Cheyenne."

"Hell, yes, I mind."

"Excuse me?" Taken aback, Hannah frowned and stepped aside as Devin swung over the fence, leaving the colt to thrust its head over the top rail, nuzzling his shirt, as if it had forgotten all about trying to bury Devin in the dirt.

"There's no sense in you driving when you're not feeling well. You and Justin can ride up with me and C.J."

"What makes you think I'm not feeling well?" Hannah bluffed.

"You've gotten sick almost every morning since I came here," Devin said dryly. "I figured the odds are in favor of it."

Smart-ass. Hannah resisted the urge to swallow the salty taste in her mouth. "I prefer to have my own transportation home. You might meet up with friends, want to celebrate..."

"I'll take that as a vote of confidence. But I don't plan on any partying, win or lose, if that's what you're worried about."

That was it exactly, and Hannah stared at her boots, recalling the times she'd found herself stuck after some rodeo, waiting for Travis. Or worse yet, drawn into the midst of his celebration.

"Travis like to party?" Devin asked gently.

Hannah's cheeks burned at his knowing gaze. "The few times I went to the rodeo with Travis, it seemed so. I got pregnant—and sick—so soon after we were married that I usually stayed home. After Justin was born it seemed best not to go. Besides, there were chores to be done...."

"It won't be that way with me, Hannah." Devin's husky voice promised that all kinds of things might be different with him. Then he added, "I'll have C.J. along to keep my partying to a minimum."

There was truth to his words, but Hannah couldn't help recalling that C.J.'s presence hadn't kept Devin from celebrating at Greeley. Hadn't kept him from kissing her....

"I appreciate the gesture, but really, I feel...I feel..." She felt sick, and she shoved her purse and cookies into Devin's arms.

"Hannah..."

Ignoring Devin's concern and his exasperation, Hannah cupped her hand over her mouth and dashed to the house.

Minutes later she bathed her face with a cool cloth and brushed her teeth. Her nausea had passed, but she felt no more like driving to Cheyenne than she did doing jumping jacks. Still, she *had* to talk to Travis. If only Tilly had been able to wrangle a day off. But Tilly hadn't, and that left only Devin to turn to. Hannah sighed. All things considered, she'd be a fool to turn down his offer of a ride.

Going back outside, Hannah found Devin leaning against his truck, his arms folded, one booted foot crossed over the other. He'd tossed her belongings on the pickup's passenger seat and his smoky dare told her he anticipated her argument, maybe even looked forward to it. That helped take out some of the sting as she told him, "I've decided to accept your offer."

"I'm glad to hear it." Devin pushed up his hat brim. "You are one stubborn woman, Hannah Reese."

She smirked. "Thank you."

Devin grinned then, and a warm friendly feeling came over Hannah that made her grin back. There was a flattering respect in Devin's eyes and a whole lot of fun, neither of which she could ever recall knowing with Travis. Looking back, her days with Travis had held an uncertainty, an intensity about them, with her always hoping, wishing or worrying in one way or another.

The boys came from the barn then, and C.J. stiffened at the sight of his father smiling down at her. Hannah's good feeling faded somewhat. If Devin noticed his son's disapproval, he gave no sign, telling the boys, "Looks like we're all making this rodeo together. You boys ready?"

"I'm ready. I peed in the stall." Justin made his announcement with pride over this latest rite of passage into manhood, most likely picked up from C.J. Hannah sighed, making a mental note to discuss barn etiquette with her son later on.

But with Devin's deep chuckle, her sigh lodged in her throat. Hannah realized she was going to spend the day at the mercy of Devin's low sexy laugh, not to mention that covetous look that always found its way into his eyes when they were together.

But C.J. was already hoisting Justin onto the back seat of Devin's pickup, a long-suffering expression on his face. Much as it would have pleased C.J. to have her change her mind again, Hannah climbed in, too, blaming her indecision on hormone imbalance due to her pregnancy.

Hannah turned in the bucket seat. Justin had arranged himself on the back seat in the same slouch as C.J., pushing his hat into the same cocked position as the older boy's. "Justin, you have to buckle your seat belt."

But Justin scooted up in the seat, instead, wrapping his arms around her neck. Hannah rested her cheek against his, knowing his exuberance stemmed from making this journey with Devin and C.J., not from the knowledge he'd see his father today. Once this rodeo was over, she was going to have to put more effort into separating their lives from Devin's before her son got hurt.

Justin squirmed and Hannah reluctantly let go of him, suddenly aware C.J. watched intently. C.J. averted his gaze, but there was no mistaking the pain in his eyes, his thoughts, no doubt, on his mother, making comparisons that clearly hurt him. Hannah felt a surge of anger toward Jolene and struggled against the urge to hug C.J., as well, certain he would be appalled.

Instead, she passed C.J. his pay and cookies, thanking him for a job well-done. Devin folded his long

length into the truck and they were soon on their way
to Cheyenne. Hannah thought that between her ex and
Devin's, it promised to be a long day.

But they made the hour-plus trip smoothly, Devin
driving toward Greeley, then taking the highway
north to Cheyenne. Hannah felt better with each passing mile. Once they arrived, Devin suggested she and
Justin come along while he and C.J. checked on his
horse, taking her aside to point out that Travis might
be around.

Indeed, there were cowboys and cowgirls every-
where, many of the former competing in the slack
rodeo held mornings to cope with the overflow of
contestants. But Hannah didn't see Travis anywhere.
Judging by C.J.'s long face, Jolene wasn't here, either.

Justin begged to watch the calf roping going on in
the arena, and Hannah promised he could as soon as
he'd had breakfast. Devin opted to join them, and
Hannah couldn't stem the pleasure she felt at the prospect of Devin's company. C.J.'s obvious resentment
promised to keep things in hand.

As they walked among the milling cowhands toward one of the food stands, motherly instinct had
Hannah checking to be sure Justin remained close by.
But a different kind of caution came over her as she
surveyed the three dark-haired males escorting her,
their hands tucked into their jeans pockets, their black
hats cocked rakishly. The boys could have passed for
brothers, C.J. wearing the sulky face of a teen stuck
with his younger sibling. And it stunned her how eas-

ily she'd fallen into step alongside Devin, so closely that the flared skirt of her jumper brushed his jeans-clad leg. There seemed something intimate in the way she and Devin almost but not quite touched, something that reminded her of her parents....

"I'd like to check the draw before I eat, if you wouldn't mind walking over to the office," Devin said.

"I want to do that," Justin insisted as Hannah slowed, then stopped. She sighed. Justin didn't even understand what Devin was going to do; he just knew he wanted to go with him. Then she noticed Justin's raised voice had drawn attention. People glanced at them in passing, smiling at the boys, then at her and Devin. Hannah knew they saw the same image of family that she feared Justin might come to feel. Distancing herself and Justin from Devin and his son couldn't wait until after the rodeo.

"I think Justin and I will go ahead and find a place to sit," Hannah said swiftly.

"I can check the draw later," Devin said with a shrug, then he grinned and added, "Might spoil my appetite, knowing which bronc I have to ride."

Catching her lip, Hannah glanced about self-consciously, wondering how Devin missed the curiosity they elicited among his peers. Devin caught the eye of a fellow roper, the cowboy greeting them each in turn, then shooting Devin a speculative grin. Hannah knew by the way Devin's grin faltered that he finally realized the picture they made, the notice they'd drawn.

But Devin only frowned down at her, and Hannah tensed, aware he could be as stubborn as she. She placed a deliberate hand on Justin's shoulder, calling his attention to Justin's adoration and C.J.'s resentment.

Devin hesitated, then backed off, saying with a reluctance that made Hannah ache, "Maybe you're right. The office might be crowded. C.J. and I will meet you back here in a while."

"Fine." Hannah told herself it was relief she felt at his putting the boys first. She busied herself placating Justin as Devin and C.J. walked away.

"How about some pancakes?" Hannah suggested. But Justin stood gazing after Devin, his lower lip thrust out in a pout. "I want to go with Devin."

"Devin has work to do. And you need to have breakfast."

"I don't want breakfast." Justin's lip trembled and Hannah cursed her softheartedness where her son was concerned. She had to be strong if she didn't want Justin's heart broken.

But she wasn't hungry now, either, and she offered, instead, "Let's go over by that gate and watch the slack rodeo."

Justin was agreeable to that, but Hannah didn't miss the way he kept turning from the roping going on in the arena to watch for Devin and C.J. Once, as he lingered in his search for Devin, Hannah turned to look, too, unable to stem a flutter of anticipation. But it wasn't Devin walking her way. It was Travis. Naturally he wasn't alone.

The brassy-haired buxom cowgirl with one hand pushed into Travis's hip pocket seemed to serve more as a crutch than as Travis's usual "ornament," despite her rhinestones and fringe, for Travis leaned heavily on her, no doubt suffering the effects of a night of partying. Hannah realized that while Travis was headed straight toward her and Justin, he hadn't recognized her or his son yet. She waited, anticipating his surprise when he saw her. But her cheeks burned a little as she realized the cowgirl accompanying him was one of Travis's past flirtations.

Travis finally made eye contact. She was a woman; it was inevitable. As expected, recognition of her served as a cold splash of water in the face of what indeed appeared to be a hangover, judging by Travis's bloodshot brown eyes.

Savoring the moment, Hannah gave him a false sweet smile. "Hello, Travis."

"Well, well. Guess I don't have to ask what brings you here, Hannah." Travis recovered his composure handily, but then, Hannah thought bitterly, he'd had plenty of practice. She almost felt sorry for the cowgirl when Travis abruptly dismissed her.

Aware that Justin had inched close to her side, she caught hold of his hand and squeezed gently. Travis grinned down at their son and asked, "Did you come to see your daddy win the bronc ride today?"

Hannah felt Justin curl his small hand tightly about hers and for a moment forgot that she'd brought him here for that very purpose, caught by the urge to shield him from Travis, instead. But Justin's reply came clearly and with a stubbornness she knew was inherited when he insisted, "C.J. said Devin's going to win."

Travis chuckled, but his expression was decidedly humorless, even more so when, from a few yards behind him, Devin said with false cordiality, "C.J. is prone to exaggeration. But I do believe I'll win the calf roping today."

Hannah clenched her teeth as Devin and C.J. sauntered over. She didn't need Devin baiting her ex when she intended to pry some money out of him.

But there was purpose in Devin's step and a hard glint in his eyes. When he shot her a questioning glance, Hannah shook her head curtly, raising Justin's hand meaningfully in hers. She didn't want her son to witness an argument between Devin and Travis, didn't need Devin intervening on her behalf.

Travis wasn't cooperating, either, facing Devin boldly for a man who owed Devin tens of thousands of dollars. "I guess all that practicing I heard you been getting in my arena is paying off." Travis lowered his voice, but his words seemed to hang in the air when he added, "Movin' right in on what's mine, aren't you, Bartlett?"

Devin hooked his thumbs in his front jeans pockets. "The way I understand it, none of it's yours anymore, Reese."

Hannah silently groaned, their blatant innuendo making it clear they referred to more than livestock. Travis didn't want her, but he was prideful enough that he didn't want anyone else having her, either.

And Devin hadn't exactly made clear that training horses was his only interest at her ranch, none of which was lost on a noticeably silent C.J.

Impatient with both Travis and Devin, Hannah told them, "You men can talk rodeo later. Travis, I thought you might like to spend time with Justin today. And I need to discuss some things with you."

Travis rubbed his unshaven jaw in an evasive gesture Hannah recognized well. She stared him down mercilessly. But Travis was well up to the challenge.

"I've got to go tend to my horse right now. I'll look you up later, Hannah." Travis lifted one corner of his mouth in a smile that had once charmed her but now only left her cold. "We'll have us a drink over old times."

"I don't want a drink. But I *have* to talk to you."

"Stick around, then, and let the boy watch his daddy win a trophy buckle."

"C.J. said Devin's going to win," Justin repeated tenaciously.

"Yeah, well, we'll see about that. Catch you later, kid." With that, Travis pushed past Devin, who gave no ground. Hannah thought they were both bull-headed. But most of all she thought how she still had to tell Travis about the baby. A baby he wouldn't want any more than he wanted Justin.

Sudden tears stung her eyes. Travis had never really loved her at all.

But she didn't love him anymore, either. She blinked away her tears, drawing strength from that knowledge.

"Where's he going?" Justin asked, and they all gazed after Travis, who was headed in the opposite direction of the barn and the horse he supposedly had to tend to.

Justin sounded curious, rather than hurt by the fact that his father didn't have time to spend with him. More troubling, Hannah realized, was the way Justin didn't want to let Devin out of his sight.

"He's just...busy," Hannah finally explained. The sun had climbed in the sky and seemed to beat down on her as relentlessly as the worries that plagued her. Devin turned to her then, and Hannah knew she had only to ask his help in dealing with Travis. But she was determined to handle this alone. And she wasn't about to let Travis put a damper on this day at the rodeo for her son.

But before she could divert Justin, C.J. said to him, "You may as well come with me. I got to go clean that horse's stall."

"Okay." Belatedly Justin asked, "Can I, Mommy?"

C.J. hooked his thumbs in his jeans pockets in impatient imitation of Devin, unaware, Hannah realized, that he'd just totally won her heart. She hadn't missed the knowing look in his eyes as he'd gazed after Travis, no doubt reliving times his mother had let him down in a similar manner.

"Sure you can," Hannah told her son. She waited until she'd caught C.J.'s attention to add, "Thank you, C.J."

He only shrugged and the boys set off.

"Kind of grows on you, doesn't he?" Devin teased, making Hannah smile, even as she hoped her heart wasn't always so plain on her sleeve. As the boys headed toward the barn, he called after them, "We'll be along shortly."

Hannah sobered then, Devin's worry about C.J. evident as his gaze lingered on his son. Guessing the source of his concern, she asked, "Is C.J. likely to meet up with Jolene?"

"The barrel races ended last night, but I expect she'll be here to watch the bull riding." Devin scrubbed his hand along his clean-shaven jaw, his frustration obvious. "Jolene hasn't wanted C.J. around all week. But she's after support money, so there's no telling what she might do after the rodeo's over. She's got time coming with C.J. and I'm afraid she's going to take it."

In that moment it was difficult for Hannah to remember there were reasons not to take Devin's hand, not to offer him comfort. "Maybe C.J. won't want to go with her."

"He'll want to go," Devin said grimly.

There was nothing she could do or say. But as Hannah turned with Devin toward the barn, she was once again overcome by a feeling of closeness that reminded her of her parents.

Despite their earlier attempts to avoid it, they wound up having breakfast together. Devin seemed caught up in worry about what Jolene would do, and Hannah no longer had the heart to protest when he herded them to the food stand. Walking the carnival midway seemed to naturally follow, Hannah promising herself that after today, she would gradually draw herself and Justin away from Devin and his son.

When it was time for Devin to ready himself and his horse for the day's events, he surprised Hannah with tickets to the grandstand, promising they were good seats. She thanked him and wished him luck, but it wasn't until the rodeo started that she discovered just how good those seats were. As a red bronc was loaded into the chute directly below her and Justin, Hannah suffered a shiver that was part thrill, part chill. She could see the horse brace its legs, the whites of its eyes showing as the single-handed rigging was strapped around its belly. Hannah all but jumped from her seat when the horse whinnied, drowning out the announcer's introduction of the first bareback rider.

Most of the bucking horses she'd ever watched had continued kicking even after dislodging their riders. Bronc riding had never seemed much safer than bull riding to her. She wondered how tough a bronc Devin had drawn.

"Dad drew No Glory." C.J. plunked himself down in the seat next to Justin, startling Hannah. His presence was no doubt a command appearance compliments of Devin. C.J. seemed to take to the role of commentator, however, looking the part in his PRCA T-shirt and sounding it as he went on to explain, "You know, 'no guts, no glory.' Horse has only been ridden a few times this year. He bucks real hard. Dad will get a good score if he can ride him."

"Devin can ride him," Justin said loyally.

Hannah sincerely hoped so.

When the first horse threw its rider into the arena fence, Hannah gasped in dismay, along with nine-tenths of the crowd.

"You land where you look," C.J. said, unruffled, as if the rider should have known better.

"Devin can beat him," Justin said, as if he knew better, too.

Travis climbed on a horse in chute number three, and Hannah leaned forward in her seat. Trying to muster some enthusiasm for her son, she told Justin, "There's your daddy."

Mostly Hannah noticed that Travis was wearing new fringed red leather chaps she knew had to cost a pretty penny.

Justin said nothing, only watched the ride, then looked to C.J. for the critique that had been forthcoming after the first two bronc rides.

C.J. glanced warily at Hannah. She waited, too, and seeing that she did, C.J. told them, "He didn't get his bronc spurred out. But the judges won't count it against him because the horse balked before leaving the chute—he'll get a free roll."

Hannah thought that sounded typical of Travis.

C.J. added for Justin's benefit, Hannah was sure, "He did okay for a bad draw. Dad's next."

Hannah was on the edge of her seat this time. Devin was resplendent in his black shirt and hat, wearing a flashy pair of purple-and-black fringed chaps with his initials on each leg. He shoved down his hat and Hannah held her breath as he adjusted his rigging, easing himself onto the black horse, which shifted and snorted, trying to rub Devin against the side of the chute. Devin raised himself slightly, then hunkered down on the horse's back, his gloved hand secure in his rigging. He gave a quick nod. Before Hannah was ready, the horse burst from the chute.

Devin cut an arc in the air with his arm in perfect timing to the rhythm of his spurring, his chaps flapping, the fringe flying as his legs worked forward over the horse's shoulders, then back toward the rigging with each buck. Sun flashed on Devin's silver spurs. Horse and rider struck perfect harmony even as they strove to best the other.

The buzzer sounded. Devin slipped neatly from his bucking mount onto the pickup horse, then dropped gracefully from its back to his feet. He lifted his hat briefly in response to the enthusiastic crowd, his shiny black hair plastered to his forehead, his grin creasing his bronzed face. Hannah's madly beating heart seemed to still as she realized in that moment just how much Devin was willing to give up for his son.

Devin's gaze burned brightly their way, then he turned to collect his rigging. The boys quit whooping and hollering to catch Devin's score, then whooped and hollered again when it ranked him second. They'd settled down some by the time Devin wound up in fourth place. Hannah deliberately shifted her thoughts from Devin to the grim fact that Travis hadn't made any money thus far today, which was all the excuse he needed not to pay child support.

"C.J.'s mom rides horses, too."

Justin imparted this knowledge in a tone that said he was clearly impressed, innocently unaware that he'd left Hannah feeling suddenly inadequate, as if riding a horse was a natural attribute of motherhood.

"I've always wanted to learn to ride," she told him, hoping that somehow raised her worth in his eyes.

"You live on a ranch. And you've got a horse." C.J. couldn't seem to resist pointing that out. "But you can't ride?"

"I always wanted a horse when I was young, but I never had one. After I married and moved onto the ranch, I was busy with Justin—he was only a baby. And later Travis...well, Travis couldn't teach me because he was busy, too."

C.J. regarded her far too knowingly for a twelve-year-old, then gazed back over the arena being readied for the calf-roping event. After a moment he said grudgingly, "My dad could probably teach you. Hell—heck, he taught me to ride when I was just a kid."

So there might even be hope for me, Hannah thought wryly. Still, she was struck by that urge to hug C.J. again, suspecting he was warming to her whether he wanted to or not. Hannah had to admit the idea of Devin teaching her to ride held appeal. Too much appeal.

Hannah kept her reply noncommittal. "I'll keep that in mind, C.J. Now, how would you boys like a cold drink? My treat?"

The boys were thirsty. Hannah stood, welcoming

the breeze that reached her, realizing just how warm the afternoon was. "Why don't you stay and watch? I need to stretch my legs, anyway."

And she needed to clear her mind of the idea of Devin teaching her anything. She'd already learned his kiss was sweet enough to make her head spin. That was all she needed to know.

Hitching her purse strap over her shoulder, she made her way to a concession stand. Finding a long line of customers, she turned back and decided to try again later. She had no intention of missing the calf roping.

She skirted the crowd in her effort to hurry, only to find Travis watching her from a short distance away, his gaze drawn to where the breeze molded her denim dress to her belly. She slowed her steps, walking over to him. Their talk could be put off no longer.

Travis's nostrils flared, revealing a tension his nonchalant voice belied. "Well, well. That Devin's baby you're carrying?"

Hannah felt a pang, knowing he hoped it was, feared it wasn't. But she was through with regrets over "what might have been" with Travis. "This is your baby, Travis. This is what I came to tell you."

"Dammit, Hannah." Travis gripped her arm. "Why'd you let that happen?"

"I didn't think I could get pregnant any more than you did!" Hannah flushed, wishing they were farther from the crowd. She lowered her voice to tell him, "The fact is, it happened, that last time just before the divorce. You might try making the best of it and enjoy your children.''

His grip on her arm tightened, but Hannah refused to give Travis the satisfaction of a struggle. It was his scathing words that hurt most. ''If I'd known you'd get pregnant, I would never have come by that night.''

Before Hannah could muster a comeback, Devin said from behind her, ''Get your hands off her, Reese.''

Hannah swung around, almost losing her balance as Travis let go of her in the same moment she pulled free. Her heart caught in her throat at the menacing look in Devin's eyes. He held iced drinks from the concession stand and moisture dripped from the paper cups, a muddy pool gathering atop one of his dusty boots. Shame heated her cheeks with the realization that he must have overheard how Travis had used her.

''I can handle this, Devin,'' she said. ''We're just talking.''

Both men ignored her.

''This isn't your business, Bartlett,'' Travis warned, taking a bold stride forward.

''I'm making it mine.'' Devin tossed the drinks aside, his step determined.

''Devin, no!'' Hannah clutched his arm. It was the wrong thing to do. Travis let go with an uppercut to Devin's jaw that dropped him to the ground.

Chapter Seven

Devin saw stars.

His jaw ached and he tasted blood on his lip.

Then he remembered Travis had hit him.

And he realized it wasn't stars he was seeing from his prone position, but rays from the sun, which was blocked by a silhouette of curls that belonged to Hannah. Devin blinked, bringing her into focus, noting he'd drawn a small gathering of fellow wranglers who stood over him like he'd been laid to rest.

But his attention centered on Hannah. There was no mistaking that she was angry with him. Her gaze seared him, and Devin thought with indignation that it was Travis she ought to be mad at. It was clear Travis had used her in more ways than just leaving her to do chores while he hit the rodeo and party circuit. The thought had Devin curling his hands into fists as he pushed himself off the dirt into a sitting position.

Travis, of course, was nowhere in sight.

Hannah crouched beside him, digging a tissue from the little black purse she carried. "Your lower lip is bleeding."

Devin thought it didn't sting as much as her disapproval.

"He sucker punched you, Dev," one cowboy commiserated.

"No matter," another drawled. "There'll be a next time."

Hannah's glare had the group of cowboys dispersing.

"Better dust off and come on," one brave cowboy called back. "You got a calf waiting."

But Devin let Hannah tend to his lip. Her hands were gentle and her expression softened to one of concern that he just sat back and enjoyed. Wispy curls lay against her pink cheeks and at her temples, loosened from the clasp of pearls fastened in her hair. He liked that she'd worn the denim dress she'd been wearing the first time he kissed her. It draped over her bent knees, but didn't completely conceal her smooth legs above her black boots. Devin grinned to think a combination of denim and pearls could stir him so.

"There's nothing funny about this." Hannah stopped dabbing at his lip to give him a fresh frown. "What were you thinking, starting a fight with Travis? How am I supposed to talk with him now?"

Devin lost his grin abruptly. He didn't want Hannah talking to Travis, didn't want Travis touching her. "Travis seemed more inclined to manhandle you than talk."

"He wasn't going to hurt me. Travis has never raised a hand to me. He just—" Hannah struggled for words unsuccessfully, and tears glinted in her eyes.

"He's hurt you, Hannah. Maybe not the kind of hurt that shows, but he's hurt you."

"Well, he can't hurt me anymore." Hannah dashed the tears from her eyes and Devin silently cheered her. "What about you? How are you supposed to get your money from Travis now that you've got him mad at you?"

Devin wanted to smile at her naïveté. Hell, the first day of the rodeo he'd let Travis know with just a look that there was unfinished business between them. He'd have his money or his horse and that was all there was to it.

But he knew Hannah's problems with Travis weren't so easily solved, despite her determination. And with each passing day he wanted more to take care of those problems for her. Knowing Hannah would take exception to the notion, he simply assured her, "I can handle Travis. Maybe not with one hand tied behind my back—"

"I'm not apologizing for that, Devin Bartlett. You had no business getting into a fist fight with Travis."

Although he thought differently, Devin only reminded her dryly, "I never exactly got in on the fight, Hannah."

Pleased with the reluctant curve of her lips, Devin shook the dust from his hair, retrieved his hat from where it had fallen and jammed it on his head. He climbed to his feet, pulling Hannah along.

They stood close, dusty boot to boot, denim brushing denim, his hat brim shading Hannah's sun-kissed face. He'd curled his hands about her arms and found he wasn't inclined to let go of her, enjoying the feel of her soft skin over sturdy little muscles. He could sense the caution that came over her, though, in the way her smile slipped. Still, she kept looking at his mouth.

Encouraged, he murmured, "I think my lip requires a little more first aid. Something warm and soft..."

Devin soothed himself with a gentle kiss that lasted just long enough for Hannah's lashes to flutter down, but not long enough to draw undue attention he knew would upset her. The kiss made her sigh and made him hungrier for her, but he released her. He had to.

Hannah settled her purse strap over her shoulder, and Devin noticed her hands trembled slightly. She glanced about self-consciously, but all she said was, "You've got a calf waiting, remember?"

"I'll rope him in record time now." Devin grinned.

"The boys are counting on that." Hannah's smile faded quickly with the mention of their children. She was probably reminded, the same as he, of all the reasons they shouldn't be kissing. He was sure of it when she brought her hand to rest over the baby she carried. "I'd better get back to the grandstand."

After she'd gone, Devin stood for a moment,

weighing those reasons against the needs and wants churning inside him. He recalled Hannah cheering from the stands after his bronc ride, all sparkly-eyed and breathless, their boys whooping it up alongside her. There'd been something…right in the way that moment had made him feel. Something that had him envisioning a life that revolved around Hannah, the children, the ranch and the rodeo.

Devin reminded himself it was a life he'd envisioned before. But he couldn't let go of the image. And he couldn't forget the possessive feeling that had gripped him when he'd heard Travis ask Hannah if her baby belonged to Devin. These thoughts stayed with him even as he turned his attention to beating Travis in the roping competition.

Victory wasn't as sweet as Hannah's kiss, but it was the next best thing. He hadn't won the event, but he'd outroped Travis and that seemed all that mattered. Travis hadn't made any money, however, and Devin knew that didn't bode well for Hannah in terms of child support. Figuring she would come looking for Travis, he decided to wait at the barn for her and the boys. Hannah wouldn't take the news well that Travis's horse and gear were already gone.

Devin went to hitch the truck and trailer, then drove over and parked near the barn with the intention of loading his gear. He was confident the California cowboy would be by to purchase his horse.

As he climbed from the truck, Devin caught a glimpse of Hannah's denim dress and shiny curls just inside the door. The boys weren't in sight, and the barn area was quiet, the saddle bronc event having drawn most cowboys to the arena. But Hannah wasn't alone. Recognizing the flash of red satin over familiar curves, Devin closed the truck door with a quiet click and started slowly over, filled with the caution of a man about to step between a woman he'd had and a woman he wanted.

It had been a month since he'd seen Jolene. She'd come by the place he'd leased in Sedalia, bringing C.J. home early from a weekend visit despite all her talk about custody and child support. She'd had a rodeo to go to and another man to go with her. C.J. would have been in the way, the same as he would have been here at Cheyenne. But the rodeo was over now, and Devin tensed, wondering what Jolene had up her white-fringed red-satin sleeve.

Always a showy dresser, Jolene was no less so today, the fringe hanging from all the right places, the satin clinging. Her long black hair hung down her back below the brim of a pricey red hat. It was easy to understand how she'd once made his heart beat faster. But he wondered how he'd missed her cold heart beneath all the frills, or the selfishness in her dark eyes.

Neither woman seemed to notice his approach, and Devin stepped off to the side of the barn door, curiosity mixing with his caution.

"You must be Hannah, the one who bakes cookies," Jolene was saying, no doubt making the connection as Hannah waited by his gear. C.J. had apparently been talking to his mother about Hannah, favorably so, considering Jolene's condescending tone. Devin knew Jolene's attitude had everything to do with her womanly pride and nothing to do with C.J. Jolene was probably trying to put two and two together where he and Hannah were concerned.

But then, so was he.

"I'm Hannah Reese."

Devin recognized the chill in Hannah's voice. She didn't seem the least intimidated by Jolene's forward manner, yet he felt a surge of protectiveness for her. Jolene wasn't above a catfight. And while he'd bet his horse on Hannah, there was the fact that she was pregnant to consider. Jolene's next words made it clear that fact hadn't escaped her notice.

"C.J. didn't mention you were pregnant. Just that Dev had leased your barn."

Though she wasn't as blatant as Travis, there was a wealth of speculation in Jolene's voice.

"C.J. doesn't know I'm pregnant. I haven't told many people yet."

"I imagine Devin's noticed," Jolene said knowingly. Glancing inside Devin saw her place her hands on her trim waist in a deliberate way, her fingers splayed to emphasize her flat stomach. He was filled with disgust.

"Yes, Devin's…noticed."

Devin was certain the warmth showing on Hannah's cheeks came from the memory of him finding the mound of her belly with his hand as he kissed her. He felt the heat of that memory, as well…

"I reckon plenty of folk took note today, what with Travis and Devin fighting over you."

Devin grimaced, nursing his tender jaw with his hand, though he wasn't surprised Jolene had heard; news traveled fast and far among rodeo folk. That Jolene wondered what the fight had been over was clear.

"Devin and Travis just had a misunderstanding," Hannah quickly explained, probably hoping to stave off further speculation on Jolene's part.

"Maybe that's because Dev finds your setup so appealing. Travis left you sitting real pretty on that ranch."

Devin winced, knowing Hannah would take offense at the notion Travis had given her anything. And Hannah had to know by now that he found more than her "setup" appealing. But before Hannah could react, Jolene went on, "Settled life seems to suit you. I'm concentrating on my career myself, now that my son is grown."

Pushing thirteen wasn't "grown." Devin wanted to spit the words out. And he was sure Jolene didn't measure her success on just her performance in the arena.

"I've always wanted to learn to ride," Hannah confessed, surprising Devin even as he struggled to rein in his temper. Then Hannah knocked the wind out of him by saying, "Devin's going to teach me after the baby is born."

Devin rolled his gaze skyward. He wondered if Jolene would see the lie in Hannah's eyes as easily as he once had. He mentally promised to teach Hannah to ride, as if by doing so she wouldn't be lying and there would be nothing for Jolene to see.

His ploy seemed to work, for Jolene warned Hannah, "Dev won't stay off the circuit long enough for that, honey. Rodeo gets in a man's blood—the same way a woman gets in a man's blood."

Women. Devin hadn't realized they fought so dirty. Even Travis's sucker punch had been cleaner than this. Before Jolene filled Hannah's head with nonsense about her still being in his blood, which was threatening to boil right now, Devin stepped into the barn. His temper mellowed some with the humorous sight of the two surprised faces that greeted him.

Caught in her lies, Hannah's cheeks burned bright. Caught scheming, Jolene adopted a cloying manner with practiced ease. "Dev, honey, I just met your friend. C.J. tells me you're leasing her barn."

"That's right." Devin braced himself as Jolene sidled up close, giving her long hair a shake that had it rippling snakelike down her back.

"Better watch out for Travis Reese. I hear he's got a mean streak."

"It ain't Travis's mean streak I'm worried about," Devin said, looking her straight in the eye. He didn't so much as blink when she gave a false laugh, brushing her body against his in passing as she headed for the door.

Devin didn't turn to watch her go. He'd seen that act a thousand times. Rather, he enjoyed Hannah's pink cheeks, the glitter in her eyes revealing the heat was due more to pique than embarrassment now.

"So, that's your ex-wife."

"Yeah. That's Jolene." With luck, that was the last he'd see of her this trip. Devin took a step closer to Hannah. She held her ground admirably, although the color in her cheeks blossomed anew. "So, you want to learn to ride."

"I've always wanted to learn to ride."

"You haven't always wanted me to teach you."

Devin took another step and this time Hannah retreated a step, as well. Two more steps had her back to the wall. Devin braced his hands on either side of her face, noting the awareness in her silky-lashed eyes, the quick breaths passing between her rosy lips. He leaned closer, compelled by an aching need. "Is that all you want from me, Hannah?"

Hannah closed her eyes and whispered, "I don't know."

He knew. Devin lowered one hand, toying with the top button of her denim dress. "Did Travis buy you this dress?"

Hannah opened her eyes at the gritty sound of his voice. His penetrating gaze had her answering on a quick rush of breath, "No."

She knew Devin would have kissed her then, but the boys could be heard outside the barn, Justin's two-step trying to keep pace with C.J.'s lanky stride. She and Devin moved apart as the boys walked inside the barn, but not quickly enough, judging by C.J.'s suspicious frown.

Justin greeted them, then turned his attention to Devin's horse. But C.J. spotted Devin's split lip and his frown was replaced by a concern that tugged at Hannah's heart. As she wondered how Devin would explain the injury, C.J.'s frown returned and he demanded, "Who hit you, Dad?"

C.J. apparently recognized the evidence of a fight when he saw it.

Devin cast a pointed glance in Justin's direction. But Justin appeared oblivious, busy trying to charm Devin's horse over to the stall door to be petted. "Travis and I had a disagreement."

"Bet you showed him." C.J.'s confidence had Hannah wincing along with Devin. Then C.J. poured salt on the wound by asking, "Do we get Jet back now?"

"Our disagreement wasn't about the horse, C.J."

"Then what were you fighting about?"

Devin glanced at her, clearly at odds at how to explain. But that one look her way apparently said it all for C.J. With unflattering disbelief, he challenged, "You got in a fight over *her?*"

"C.J.!" Devin all but hissed at his son and Hannah's heart sank. Whatever warmth C.J. had come to feel for her had iced over now. And she was certain Devin lost favor, as well, as he explained with reluctance to C.J., "It wasn't exactly a fight. Travis caught me off guard with a punch."

"He *beat* you in a fight?" C.J.'s struggle to comprehend had Hannah feeling sorry for Devin even as she hoped C.J.'s high expectation of his father was based on his hero worship, not past altercations. Seemingly it was a little of both, for C.J. said accusingly to Devin, "You told me never to get in a fight unless it's important. And if it's important enough to fight over, it's important enough to win."

Devin took the verbal blow without flinching, but Hannah could see he was disturbed by his son's disapproval. While she didn't want to give the impression she condoned fighting, she knew she had to tell C.J. how Travis had managed to overpower Devin. "C.J., it was my fault—"

"This is all your fault!" C.J. backed away, his eyes glittering with tears. Hannah tried not to be hurt, understanding his resentment of her, but still, his anger stung.

"We'll talk about this later in private." Devin's low voice carried a warning, and Hannah realized Justin now watched them with wide wary eyes.

"I don't want to talk about anything." C.J. took another step back. "I just saw Mom. She said I can come with her for a while." C.J. drew a deep breath. "I'm going."

Long seconds passed as Devin gazed at his son. Hannah could all but see the hurt that passed between them, their shoulders hunched with it, the pain bright in their eyes. Devin said evenly, "Are you sure this is what you want to do?"

C.J. gave a curt nod.

Hannah caught her lip to hold back a protest, stunned by the strength of her protective feelings for C.J. Having met Jolene, she didn't doubt that the

woman would use her son as a means to an end that
had nothing to do with C.J.'s welfare.

Devin's nostrils flared as he dug in his hip pocket
for his wallet. He retrieved some bills and held them
out to C.J. "You'll need cash with you."

"I got money."

Devin grimly shoved the bills back in his wallet.
"Well, son, you give me a call every week to let me
know how you're doing—or if you need more money
or want me to come and get you."

"I'd better be going." But C.J. took only a couple
of steps, then turned back to Hannah. His uncertainty
was heartbreakingly obvious, despite his show of independence. "What about my job feeding your
stock?"

"If it's all right with Hannah, I can take over until
you come back," Devin told him.

C.J. glanced at his father, and for a moment Hannah feared that out of anger and disappointment C.J.
would declare he wasn't coming back.

Quickly she said, "It's fine with me."

"Thanks," C.J. muttered, and he walked out the
barn door.

Justin was off in a heartbeat, going after C.J. as
unerringly as Devin's loop sailing after a calf. Hannah
hurried to the door. Justin caught up with C.J. and
they stopped, C.J. speaking to her son a moment, then
walking on, leaving Justin to stare after him.

Devin came to stand by her shoulder. Hannah
turned to him, her frustration mounting with his quiet
countenance. "You can't just let him go!"

"I can't legally keep him from his mother. Even if I forced him to stay, it would only work against me."

She recognized then the utter devastation in the depths of Devin's eyes. She heard it in his hollow voice. She wanted to press her hand to his chest, absorb some of the pain she knew lay in his heart. He was right, of course. C.J. had to discover the truth for himself about his mother. Her throat felt tight as she asked, "Where will Jolene take him?"

"She'll head over to the rodeo in Loveland, then on down to Colorado Springs. Although if she picks up a good purse in Loveland, I doubt she'll keep C.J. with her that long. I just hope C.J. won't blame himself when Jolene disappoints him."

Devin rested his hand on her shoulder, giving a squeeze Hannah realized was meant to reassure both of them. Then he directed her attention to Justin, whose small boots dragged up dust as he shuffled toward them, a tired dusty disillusioned little cowboy.

Justin stopped before her and pushed up his hat brim in a gesture so like Devin's that Hannah's heart squeezed.

"C.J. said I can't come with him."

"He's going to visit his mother awhile," Hannah explained.

"And he's left me pretty shorthanded." Devin crouched before Justin. "Think you can help me load my gear?"

"Sure I can." Justin trotted over to Devin's duffel bag by the stall.

Hannah didn't have the heart to call him back. Instead, she said to Devin, "If you don't mind keeping an eye on Justin, I'll go find Travis and ask him about that child support."

"Travis is gone, Hannah."

It took a moment for Devin's words to register.

"That can't be. Travis hasn't even said goodbye to Justin!" Anger flared, but burned out quickly for Hannah. She'd never really expected anything different from Travis.

Until the California cowboy came by, chores helped to distract them all from C.J.'s absence. He finally showed up and bought the gelding, and Devin at least seemed pleased by that. As he shook the man's hand, Hannah heard the cowboy say, "You've got a pretty hot rope, Devin. Keep it up and you'll be roping at the finals in Vegas."

Hannah recalled C.J. predicting much the same if his father stayed on the circuit. The words struck more sharply now that she knew how much Devin loved the rodeo. Now that he'd kissed her...

"I'm mostly training horses right now," was Devin's reply, and Hannah could read nothing, good or bad, in his impassive voice.

The ride home was quiet, Justin falling asleep after the first mile, his hat clutched in his arms like some favorite stuffed toy. Hannah knew Devin's thoughts were on C.J. He'd laid his hat on the back seat, brim up, and, like Justin, his hair was flattened to his scalp like a shiny black cap. Below the glossy strands his brow was creased in worry.

As for herself, Hannah's worry seesawed from Devin and C.J. to the financial blow that came with Travis's lack of support. In comparison, her financial worries paled. At least she had her son. Hannah reached around the seat to touch Justin's hand, and as he curled his fingers instinctively around hers, she prayed Devin would soon have his son back, as well.

It was nearing sunset when they turned down the lane to the ranch, the mix of blue-violet sky and cool calm air a balm after the hot tension-filled day. Justin awoke as Devin slowed the truck, leaving the blacktop for crushed gravel. Hannah expected an argument with her son, certain Justin would want to go to the barn with Devin, instead of into the house for his bath. But once Devin parked the truck and they climbed out, Justin surprised her, leaning against her to murmur, "Carry me, Mommy."

Hannah caught her lip, brushing her hand over Justin's tousled curls. It was more than tiredness that had her son cuddling close. He was upset over C.J.'s leaving. She wanted nothing more in that moment than to gather up her little boy and hold him close. But Justin was heavy enough that she hesitated, worried about the baby she carried. She held Justin on her lap and hugged him often, but she hadn't actually hoisted him up in her arms of late.

"How about I give you that lift while your mom unlocks the door?" Justin was, of course, agreeable. Hannah met Devin's knowing gaze gratefully, aware the time had come to tell Justin about the baby.

But not tonight. Justin had had a big enough day.

She would tell him tomorrow. Maybe the prospect of a baby brother or sister would ease his disappointment over C.J.'s leaving.

They walked up to the house and Hannah opened the door, turning as Devin settled her son on his feet. Before Devin could straighten, Justin wrapped his arms around Devin's neck in a hug. Hannah's heart ached for her son, for she knew his feelings toward Devin were growing stronger despite her efforts to prevent it. If he was this upset about C.J., how would he take it when Devin and C.J. left for good? Hannah caught her breath as Justin let go with a grin and ran inside. But Devin drew himself up slowly, the pain that came into his eyes telling as his thoughts naturally turned to his son. The ache in Hannah's heart shifted inexorably toward Devin.

"Thank you, Devin."

"It was no trouble." Devin sighed softly, and Hannah sensed he wanted to linger. But he stepped from the porch, calling back to her, "Good night, Hannah."

He cut a stark silhouette against the evening sky. Hannah worried about him long after she'd gone inside and tucked Justin into bed.

As the hour grew late and lonely, Hannah sat in her kitchen with a small lamp burning over the sink. She realized she was going to miss Devin coming onto the porch at night. Miss the attention of a man by moonlight...

But those were thoughts she shouldn't be thinking.

She'd reached for the light switch, intending to go to bed, when she heard Devin's boot step on the porch.

Unexpectedly exasperation gripped her, purely feminine in its nature. He'd caught her in her pajamas again, this time pink ones that made her look like a little girl, especially with her wet hair caught up in a bright pink clip. As Devin rapped lightly on the door, Hannah contemplated removing the clip, then rejected the idea. Her hair would be a tangled mess. And where was her robe? Realizing she'd left it on the bed, she sighed, deciding the loose cotton shirt showed little enough that it didn't matter. The bottoms, as usual, spilled over her feet, revealing only her toes, adding to the little-girl image. Hannah ruefully patted her stomach. A chubby little girl.

She opened the door, and even in the dim light she noticed the bruising on Devin's jaw from Travis's punch. He'd showered and she instinctively breathed in the lingering scent of shaving cream. His hair had already dried into shiny layers, its darkness enhanced by the pale denim shirt he wore loose over his jeans.

She realized that while she savored the sight of him, Devin was looking his fill of her, too. The way his eyes heated told her there was nothing childlike in what he saw. The glide of his gaze down to her toes was familiar now, then it slipped back up, resting on the top pink button of her pajamas. That he wanted her was plain, and Hannah fervently wished in that moment that she was slim again and dressed in silk.

Then she took the wish back, her baby-to-be too precious for her to pine over her lost figure.

Plus, she knew enough of cowboys now to know Jolene was right about one thing: rodeo got in a man's blood. There wasn't a doubt in her mind that Devin would make his way back to the circuit, to the life he obviously loved. The difference was, he was a man, and the thought of leaving probably wouldn't hold him back from what he wanted....

When Devin brought his gaze back to hers, Hannah glanced away, then noted for the first time that he held Justin's hat in his hand.

"I thought Justin might miss this come morning."

"He'll likely put it on first thing."

Devin slowly handed over the hat and Hannah could all but hear him wishing C.J. was here at the ranch, safe in bed, too. She opened the door wider, moving aside, knowing this time, missing his son, Devin would come inside.

He stepped across the threshold and Hannah curled her bare toes as he passed by. She could tell he was wearing his best boots; they weren't scarred from spurs or stirrups or run down at the heel, and the tops were genuine snakeskin, a rich gray and black. They looked like the kind of boots a man might go dancing in. That made her think of the cowgirl, Shelly, and Hannah sighed inwardly, motioning Devin to the table. "I haven't been drinking coffee lately, but I have fresh lemonade."

"Sounds fine."

Hannah hung Justin's hat on the rack by the door, then went to the refrigerator for the pitcher. Devin crossed her kitchen but he remained standing, looking about the white-painted room, made cozy with green plants and yellow curtains. She hoped he didn't ask where she'd placed her dream catcher; it hung above the oak headboard of her bed.

A small vase of columbine sat centered on the long wooden table, and Devin touched a violet blossom, so gently, Hannah noticed, that it did not stir. "These are pretty."

"Justin picked them for me." Hannah smiled, setting the pitcher on the counter and taking glasses from the cupboard. "Luckily I caught him before he bared a patch of my border."

"You wouldn't have minded. Not really," Devin said knowingly, crossing over to lean on the counter and watch her pour lemonade. "Just like you don't really mind when he tracks in mud or spills lemonade."

"Or spits or uses the facilities in the stall," Hannah teased pointedly, setting the pitcher aside.

Devin's lips curved, but there was such a sadness in his eyes she knew in that moment it wasn't Justin, but C.J. he'd been talking about. Her smile faded, and seeing it did, Devin seemed to drop all pretense of good cheer. He straightened, restlessly pushing his hands into his front jeans pockets. "I can't stop thinking about C.J. I know Jolene doesn't want him, but I can't help worrying he won't come back."

"Oh, Devin." This time Hannah couldn't resist the urge she'd had earlier that day to place her hand on his chest, to share his pain, a pain all the harder to bear because there was nothing Devin could do but wait for his son to learn a tough lesson. "C.J. idolizes you. That'll bring him home sooner or later, whether Jolene wants him or not."

"I guess I have to believe that." Devin smiled ruefully. "Though I'm not so sure about the 'idolize' part."

"C.J. wants to bronc ride, like you. He told me himself the first night we met." Hannah smiled and added convincingly, "He hates baseball."

"He likes you, Hannah. He fights it, but he likes you."

"I believe so."

"And it's good to know I have a redeeming quality in his eyes. C.J. wasn't impressed that I lost a fight today."

"But he remembered what you taught him." And Hannah quoted, "'If it's important enough to fight over, it's important enough to win.'"

Devin drew his hands from his pockets. He reached up, touching her cheek with the same gentleness as he'd touched the flower. "I should have won."

Her hand was still pressed to his chest, and Hannah could feel the strong beat of his heart, all but hear it in the nighttime quiet of her kitchen. Her own heart had seemed to stop beating with his words. He traced his fingers down her cheek and along the curve of her neck, then reached with both hands to slip the clip from her hair. The strands fell damp and tangled about her shoulders. Devin lay aside the clip, weaving his fingers into her hair, his warm palms tipping her face to his.

The urgent press of Devin's mouth on hers was more than Hannah could resist. She curled both hands into his shirtfront, rising into his kiss, his lean hard body somehow accommodating the new soft roundness of hers, making her feel feminine, desirable. He lowered his hands to grip her arms, dragging her closer still. Hannah sensed his desperation and the underlying pain. He wanted to forget. And she *wanted*. But she wouldn't help him *this* way....

Hannah uncurled her fingers and flattened her palms against Devin's chest, turning her face from his.

"Hannah..." His voice was ragged and deep and almost more than she could bear.

"Let me go."

Devin held her a moment longer, a moment that took all her willpower not to melt back against him. His breath warmed her face, cooled her moist lips. When he finally took his hands from her, his gaze demanded an explanation.

She readily gave it to him. "I won't be used the way Travis used me."

Devin's anger was swift, darkening his eyes. He took a step back and the scrape of his boots on the floor was as harsh as his words when he told her, "There's a difference between being used and being needed."

Then he strode past her and out the door, pulling it shut with a definitive click that Hannah knew reflected the tight hold he had on his temper.

But she'd done the right thing. As she told herself

so, Hannah sagged against the counter, still weak-kneed from Devin's kiss. Still yearning. A lot of hurt had melted along with her defenses, and she'd found herself open to desire in a way she'd never thought to know again.

But her desire and Devin's pain weren't reason enough to have her heart broken again. She picked up the pink clip from the counter and refastened her hair. She turned out the light and made her way through the dark to her bed.

Long minutes passed. Restless, Hannah reached up and smoothed the feathers of her dream catcher. Then she curled on her side, closing her eyes. She tried not to think of Devin alone and missing his son…needing her. And she tried not to contemplate what life might be like married to a rodeo cowboy who loved her.

But she dreamed…

Chapter Eight

Sunlight streaming through her bedroom window roused Hannah the next morning. She'd overslept, proof of it in the sound of Justin's voice coming from the kitchen. He rarely awoke before her.

But if he did, he always came in to get her up. Hannah hurried out of bed, then stopped to pull on her wrapper. Unless Justin was talking to himself or on the telephone, he wasn't alone.

Hannah skimmed barefoot across the hardwood floor, down the hall and to the kitchen, her wrapper a billowing blue cloud that settled about her as she stopped in the doorway. Justin held the porch door wide and Devin filled it, looking all cowboy in his faded red shirt and jeans. Recalling his anger when he'd left her last night, Hannah eyed him warily.

"Devin said there are kittens in the barn!"

Justin's excitement was endearing and understandable to Hannah. Travis had chased off every stray cat that wandered by; he hadn't liked having pets underfoot. Whenever Tilly called to report a new batch of kittens at the guest ranch, Hannah took Justin there to see them. It was past time Justin had a kitten of his own.

But Hannah got sidetracked in telling him so, struck by the covert concern in Devin's eyes below his hat brim.

"I thought I'd take the boy to see the kittens." Devin's easy tone belied the worry she glimpsed.

"Can I, Mom? I got on my clothes already."

Hannah couldn't help a half smile. The herd of horses galloping across Justin's chest belonged on his back. But he had on his play jeans and boots, so she told him, "Sure you can. I'll be along in a few minutes."

Devin took Justin's hat from its peg and handed it to her son. "How about getting my rope from the bunkhouse for me before we head to the barn?"

"Yes, sir," Justin said, sounding so much like C.J. that Hannah was reminded of the need to avoid just such a bonding between her son and Devin. As Justin ran out the door, she vowed to herself that once they'd seen the kittens, they were coming directly back to the house.

Then Devin walked over to her, hat in hand now, his concern showing plainly and scattering her thoughts again. His voice was deep, almost tense, when he asked, "Is everything all right with the baby?"

Perplexed, Hannah rested her hand on her stomach. "Of course."

"You're usually an early riser.' Devin rotated his hat in his hands. "Even after I fed the stock, I didn't see you up and about. I got to wondering…and then I got to worrying…" Devin broke off, working his hat in his hands again. "I can see now that you're all right."

She'd felt fine until he'd come along, Hannah wanted to say. Her heart had skipped a beat with his words and there was a fever-bright glow deep inside her now. It all served as a warning, but something in the way Devin tortured his hat made her realize she'd given him a scare, and she reached out to still his hands. "I'm *fine*. The baby is fine."

Devin's hands were rough and warm, and when he turned one to capture hers, Hannah's heart stuttered again in its beat. "You're sure?"

She was sure that if she stood here letting him hold her hand, allowing that glow to flame inside her, she was asking for trouble. She slipped her hand free. "I'm sure."

And as she said so aloud, Hannah realized that she did feel fine. No wonder she'd slept so deeply. She'd awakened sick every morning for months. A glimmer of hope swept through her. "I think I might even be over my morning sickness."

"I can't say how glad I am to hear that." Before Hannah could reproach him, Devin grinned disarmingly and said, "Now you can start to enjoy being pregnant."

Then he nonchalantly pushed on his hat as if totally unaware of his charm. "You might want to bring the mama cat some food. She's feeding four babies."

"I will." Four babies. Justin would be thrilled. Enough so, that he might embrace the idea of a baby sister or brother, as well. She'd put off telling him, waiting to be sure, then waiting to tell Travis...

"Is there something else bothering you?"

Devin missed little, Hannah thought, even though his thoughts must be on C.J. "I'd planned to telephone my parents today about the baby. I was just thinking this would be a good opportunity to tell Justin, too."

"Four little kittens ought to work in your favor. How do you expect he'll take the news?"

Hannah smiled wryly. "I expect he'll have a lot of questions."

Devin chuckled. "We'll head on over to the barn. That will give you time to come up with some answers."

Hannah followed after she changed her clothes. But she felt nervous, afraid Justin would be upset about the idea of a baby. She didn't think she could take that, not on the heels of Travis's resentment. She wanted to enjoy being pregnant, just the way Devin had said.

She found Justin and Devin in an empty stall at the back of the barn, crouched in the straw to admire the kittens. She knelt beside them, setting aside two plastic bowls, one with food, one for water. Smoothing her violet maternity shirt over her belly, Hannah was amazed Justin hadn't already noticed her growing middle.

But all of Justin's attention was on the kittens, curled next to their mother in the soft nest she'd made.

"Aren't they small, Mommy?" Justin carefully stroked a sleeping kitten with his finger.

"They're adorable." Hannah sensed an opening here, and Devin's encouraging smile seemed to confirm it. "They need to be taken care of just like you did when you were small."

"Did they grow inside their mom, too?"

"Yes, she carried them there until they were ready to be born."

"Devin said these kittens are brothers and sisters. They can play together and stuff."

Judging by Justin's tone, playing together was a huge endorsement for having a brother or sister. Hannah shot Devin a grateful look that blossomed into a smile when Justin said, "I want a brother to play with, too."

"Then I have a surprise for you, Justin." Hannah took hold of his small hand and pressed it to her stomach. "You *are* going to have a baby brother or sister to play with, just in time for Christmas."

"I get a baby for Christmas?" Justin's eyes were round with wonder and he unconsciously patted her stomach. Then the wonder dimmed and he drew back his hand. "Can I still have a pony, too?"

Devin's low laugh mingled with hers, and as Hannah hugged Justin close, she realized she'd wanted, needed someone to share this moment, to later recall Justin's awe and his questions with her. She was glad that someone was Devin. "You can still have a pony if Santa has one to bring you."

"Okay, then I'll have a brother."

Hannah rolled her eyes. "I can't promise it will be a brother. It might be a sister."

"I've got a younger sister," Devin said, and Hannah looked up at him in surprise. He explained, "Debbie's a teacher in Denver. We had a lot of fun together, growing up on a farm down around Sedalia."

Hannah realized she'd only envisioned Devin as a wandering cowboy, not a man with a normal childhood and roots. Curious now, she asked, "Do your parents still live there?"

"They've retired in Arizona. We get together now and again with my sister."

"I still want a brother," Justin said, bending back over the kittens. Hannah understood the reason for his persistence when he added sadly, "I need one now that C.J. is gone."

Hannah was struck again by the worry that her son was headed for heartbreak over the Bartletts, and touched by the pain that crossed Devin's face with Justin's words. She reminded them firmly, "C.J. will be back soon."

"You're mother's right, Justin. C.J. will come back."

Devin rose and walked to the door of the stall to gaze out back of the barn. Hannah realized that his show of confidence was for Justin's sake, that he still harbored doubts about C.J.'s return.

After a moment Devin announced, "You've got riders coming."

Hannah went to stand beside Devin. "That's Tilly and Allie. They ride over from the guest ranch sometimes."

"Can I get a ride?" Justin jumped up, his unhappiness eclipsed for the moment by the prospect.

"Sure you can. Go out to the end of the fence line and wait there like always."

Justin wasted no time. Hannah's lips curved briefly in a smile, then she realized it was Devin she was attuned to now, Devin she wanted to comfort. But his gaze was distant, and she knew he no longer saw the scene before him, his thoughts with C.J. somewhere. So she only murmured, "Thanks for helping me explain things to Justin."

She half expected Devin wouldn't hear, his mind shuttered, but he gave her his full attention, gazing down at her as if committing details to memory: the shiny black band that formed her ponytail, the tiny buttons on her violet shirt. She wore her black boots, though in her condition she figured she didn't look much like a cowgirl anymore. But the warmth of Devin's smile told her he approved of what he saw.

After a moment he commented, "Justin seems keen on the idea of a baby on the ranch."

"You laid the groundwork for that pretty well. I believe Justin's going to handle having a baby around just fine."

"What about you?"

"What do you mean?" Hannah asked, puzzled.

"It won't be easy, having Justin to care for along with a newborn, plus managing the ranch. I thought, without Travis's support to count on, you might be planning to go back to your family."

Did he actually sound worried that she would go? Assuring herself that if he did, it was only due to concern about losing his lease, Hannah considered his words and said thoughtfully, "I could. Mom and Dad have always made clear that my future is secure with the café. After Travis left me, they wanted me to come back. But much as I love them, I can't turn my back on the chance to give my children everything this ranch has to offer."

"You gave up a lot for Travis."

"I got Justin and now my baby in return. Travis is the one who's going to lose out if he turns his back on his children."

"I guess I can understand how you feel."

"I know you can." Devin had given up everything for the sake of his son. He understood her better than anyone else ever could.

Devin reached out and touched her cheek.

Then Allie and Tilly trotted up on their horses outside, fine dust wafting inside the barn door along with their laughter. Devin drew back his hand, giving a rueful smile before he strode out to collect Justin. Hannah watched from the shade of the barn as the sun painted a bright picture of her son reaching out, finding a safe haven in Devin's arms. The brilliance of Justin's smile had her worrying for the first time that all she meant to give him might not be enough.

Tilly dismounted, exchanging a quick word with Devin. He took the reins from her hands and then he and Allie led both mounts toward a paddock, Justin galloping alongside. Allie's boot scuffing dejection at C.J.'s absence was obvious. And there was no missing Tilly's reproval as she turned toward the barn, her hands on her hips, her lips pursed. Apparently Justin had shared news of the baby.

"Hannah Reese, why didn't you tell me?"

"I was trying to do the right thing and inform Travis first." Hannah walked out into the sun, letting it warm away some of the coldness she still felt over Travis's resentment. "As it turns out, I may as well have told you."

"Oh, honey." All of Tilly's reproach faded, and she caught Hannah in a quick hug. "I feel terrible knowing you've dealt with this alone."

Hannah couldn't keep her gaze from slipping to where Devin and Justin helped Allie unsaddle the horses and turn them out in the paddock. Of course Tilly noticed, and she murmured speculatively, "Maybe not so alone. Devin figured things out, did he?"

Hannah wondered how long it would be before she stopped blushing over that memory. "Yes, he knows. He and C.J. have been very helpful—though before I could tell C.J. he decided to spend some time with his mother. That's hard on Devin."

Tilly sighed. "Sometimes life just isn't fair."

Reminded Tilly had suffered the loss of her husband, Hannah gave her a friend's shoulders a squeeze and quietly agreed, "No, it isn't."

"Hey, enough of this moping," Tilly scolded. "We should be celebrating."

Hannah tried to muster a smile. But her thoughts turned immediately back to Justin, to the fact that no matter how she tried, she would not always be able to shield him from hurt.

"Hannah, what is it?"

Hannah sighed. "Actually I'm trying to wean Justin away from Devin. I don't want him hurt when Devin's lease is up."

"Devin doesn't look like he's going anywhere to me," Tilly said.

Hannah had to admit there was a "settledness" to the sight of Allie and Justin sitting on the fence rail while Devin entertained them with the horses. He walked about the paddock, the untethered horses following, all but hanging their heads over his shoulder the way she'd seen his horses do. As they responded to his discreet cues to stop, back up or turn, they seemed more like docile pets than the well-trained stock horses she knew them to be. By the same token, Devin was a professional rodeo cowboy and not the contented horse trainer he appeared.

"I suppose there's the possibility that Devin might go back on the circuit," Tilly said musingly. Then she added gently, "That doesn't mean things would be the same as they were with Travis."

"There's nothing between me and Devin," Hannah

said hastily, recalling the way Devin and Tilly had taken to each other.

But there was no mistaking her relief when Tilly insisted, "Sure there is. I've seen the way he looks at you, and—" Tilly spoke quickly, saving Hannah from trying to form a protest that would be weak at best "—I've seen the way you look at him. Remember the day I brought the cookies? Devin asked me about you and Travis. That cowboy's had an interest in you right from the start."

Chagrin warmed Hannah as she recalled her jealousy that day. Tilly had likely been trying to steer Devin in her direction all along. And she remembered now Devin's asking if she thought knowledge of the baby would bring Travis home.

"Hannah, I know Travis burned you bad, but don't let that keep you from loving again. Life's too short," Tilly said knowingly.

She made it sound so simple. Made Hannah want to believe that, with Devin, anything was possible. Even marriage to a rodeo cowboy.

From across the paddock, Devin sensed something promising in the intense way Hannah watched him. At the moment, he thought it possible she might want him to stay. He knew it was only a matter of time before he would try to turn that possibility into a reality.

C.J. would come back; he would finally accept the truth that his mother didn't want him. His resentment of Hannah would fade. The time would be right then for Devin to prove to her that life with this cowboy would be everything it had never been with Travis.

But one week passed into another, and C.J. did not come back.

Chapter Nine

Devin propped his arms on the white pole fence, the horses he'd turned out to pasture milling about, nipping and giving halfhearted kicks before settling down to the business of grazing. Prairie grasses rippled golden in the evening sun, a restless movement Devin felt echo inside him.

A part of his attention seemed perpetually drawn to Hannah. He could hear the swish of the corn broom across the porch floor, hear Hannah chasten Justin, who was most likely underfoot with the old rope Devin had given him. Except for one night of rain, Hannah had swept the porch every evening since C.J. had gone, watching down the lane for his son, as if by doing so C.J. would materialize before her eyes. Devin appreciated her steadfast vigilance, his mind always on his son, whether in frustration, in worry or in prayer.

C.J. had called once to say he was on his way to Colorado Springs with Jolene. Now the rodeo in Colorado Springs was nearly over. Jolene would likely head down to Pueblo next. If she didn't send C.J. back soon or if C.J. didn't show up on his own accord, it could only mean one thing....

Devin curled his hands into fists, desperate to hang on to the hope he felt slipping.

"Devin!"

Through the misery that gripped him, Devin heard Hannah call his name, heard a catch in her voice that stopped his heart midbeat. He swung around slowly. Justin ran down the lane, his hat toppling off, gravel spitting from beneath his boots. Beyond him, a lanky boy trudged toward them, hands shoved in his jeans pockets, T-shirt hanging loose, dark hair poking from beneath his hat. A knot gathered in Devin's throat and after a moment, his burning gaze met Hannah's.

His son was home, and Devin gave thanks as he walked out to greet him.

Hannah called Justin back to the porch. Devin scooped up Justin's hat and dropped it on the little boy's head as Justin trotted by, grinning. Devin wondered if C.J. would ever appreciate the extent to which he'd been missed. Grateful for the opportunity to exchange a word alone with his son, Devin came to a halt and let C.J. take those last steps toward him. They'd parted on uneasy terms and his boy had some explaining to do.

But when C.J. stopped within arm's length, his uncertain gaze had Devin taking that last step to embrace his son. "I've missed you, C.J."

"I missed you, too, Dad." C.J. righted his hat as they stepped apart. "We still got Jet?"

"The horse is still in the barn. I doubt Travis will ever hand over any money for him," Devin reassured his son. But he wouldn't be sidetracked. "How did you get here from Colorado Springs?"

"I hitched a ride."

Devin shuddered inwardly. Outwardly he let his disapproval show. "I thought I taught you to know better than that."

"It was Charlie who gave me a ride. I'm not stupid enough to ride with strangers, Dad."

"I'm glad to hear that."

But C.J. looked a little worse for wear, and Devin started them down the lane again, thinking along the lines of food and a shower and sleep for his son. There would be time later to ask about Jolene. C.J. hadn't volunteered any information, and it wasn't hard to figure out that Jolene had found herself another traveling "companion."

As they approached the porch, C.J. seemed to tense beside him. Fingers of breeze plainly outlined Hannah's pregnancy under the pale blue T-shirt she wore, and C.J. shot him an accusing glance.

Devin bit back his exasperation. But considering Hannah didn't look very far along in her pregnancy, he made a point of explaining, "Hannah got pregnant just before she and Travis divorced."

C.J. had the grace to look sheepish and Devin fur-

ther explained, "Hannah didn't think she could have
more children—there were complications after Justin's birth. Congratulations would be in order."

"Yes, sir."

C.J.'s tone was just grudging enough to reassure
Devin he truly had back his son. When they reached
the porch, where Justin sat coiling his rope and Hannah stood waiting, C.J. said dutifully, "Congratulations on your baby."

"Thank you, C.J. I'm glad to see you."

Hannah clasped her hands and Devin knew she
fought a longing to embrace his wayward son. Her
concern was obvious and he told her, "C.J. hitched a
ride here with Charlie. Guess I owe Charlie a thanks
next time I see him."

Then he noticed C.J. shifting guiltily and sighed.
"You going to change your story on me, son?"

"No, sir. Well, maybe a little. Charlie was running
late to the rodeo in Evanston, Wyoming. I had him
drop me off this side of Greeley." Devin frowned at
that and C.J. quickly explained, "I told him I'd call
you. I just felt like walking, instead."

"You should have called me from Colorado
Springs," Devin said sternly, suspecting C.J. didn't
have a dime in his pockets. Devin masked the fear
that gripped him when he considered all the things
that could have happened to his son.

"I knew you had horses to work. And Mom
couldn't bring me because she was...busy."

Devin's temper flared. But he didn't miss C.J.'s
brief glance at Hannah, sensed some silent exchange

going on he wasn't privy to, yet found encouraging all the same.

Hannah said simply, "The important thing is that you're safe. And you're probably tired and hungry. I have apple pie and a roast ready to come out of the oven. You and your father are welcome to join us."

Justin jumped up then, his rope forgotten. "C.J. can sit by me."

Devin waited with bated breath as C.J. seemed to drink in Hannah's concern and Justin's hero worship as if he thirsted for attention. Then C.J.'s gaze moved between Hannah and Devin with a resentment so well-worn that Devin released his breath in impatience.

"I'm not hungry. Thanks, anyway," C.J. added prudently, and Devin knew his son hadn't missed his vexation. Still, C.J. said stubbornly, "I'm going down to the bunkhouse. Mom said she would call. She's making plans to pick me up by Thanksgiving."

The last was said pointedly, and Devin could all but feel Hannah's sigh of disappointment as C.J. set off for the bunkhouse. She gave Justin's shoulder a squeeze. "I'll fix a couple of plates for Justin to carry over later."

Hannah went into the house. Devin grimaced after his son, then realized he wasn't the only one who worried about C.J. Justin sat on the steps again, his rope dangling across his bent knees, his expression solemn beneath his hat brim. His sadness tugged at Devin's heart.

Devin sat down beside him. Justin's attention remained unwaveringly on C.J. His hands were curled about the rope, and Devin thought it didn't seem so long ago that C.J.'s hands had been that small.

"How about I ask your mom to send along extra pie for you to have later with C.J.?"

"Okay." Across the way, C.J. went into the bunkhouse and shut the door. Justin asked then, "When is Thanksgiving?"

This time, the tug on Devin's heart was stronger.

"It's a while yet. Lot of things can change by then."

Devin realized he'd spoken the words as much to allay his fears as to comfort Justin. When Justin went back to tossing his rope, apparently satisfied, Devin got up and walked around to the west end of the porch.

About to knock on the screened door, Devin hesitated. Hannah stood in profile near the kitchen table, tiredly rubbing the small of her back, her spine arched, her abdomen rounded, her head tipped back to ease her tension. She'd freed her hair of its ponytail and her black curls spilled about her shoulders. Her eyes were closed, and the picture she made entranced him. Tired and with child, she seemed to personify woman at her most giving.

Devin knocked softly on the door. Hannah gave a start, then smiled wearily. "Come in. I have a basket almost ready."

"Let Justin bring it. He'd like a piece of pie, too, so he can eat with C.J.," Devin added as he walked in. While Hannah busied herself with the basket, he kept on advancing. He caught her gently by the shoulders, enjoying the soft catch of her breath, then her sigh as he kneaded the hollow of her back with his hand. "Maybe you'll let up on sweeping that porch so much now that C.J. is back."

"Oh, yes…"

Devin smiled as she went limp. Nothing like a slow hand to relax a tense filly, though his efforts on her behalf had the opposite effect on him. Beneath his hand on her shoulder, he could feel the luxurious tangle of her silky curls, while her body, through her thin shirt, heated against his ministering hand. Everything warm and soft about her made him burn with tension. He wanted her, his feelings for her growing steadily deeper. Frustration worked through him with the knowledge that between her reluctance and C.J.'s resentment, he couldn't have her.

Devin managed to keep his touch light and easy, and after a moment Hannah murmured, "Devin?"

"What is it, Hannah?"

"Justin hates pie."

Devin chuckled, but as Hannah faced him, her smile fading, he reluctantly drew back his hands, reminded the same as she that Justin's hero worship could prove heartbreaking. Hannah noted wistfully, "C.J. seems as determined as ever to see his mother."

"Jolene's got a strong emotional hold on him," Devin said, tasting the bitter truth of his words. "C.J. thinks it's great she's making plans to come for him at Thanksgiving. He can't understand that's her way of saying she won't be seeing him until November."

"Jolene has hurt him. It's only natural he should want to deny it."

"It's hard, knowing she's going to let him down." Devin lowered his voice to add, "It's worse, knowing it's gotten to the point where I want her to."

"Don't let her do that to you, Devin. C.J. will eventually accept that Jolene doesn't want him with her. But that doesn't mean he'll hate her. You can't allow him to," Hannah added.

Devin lifted his hand to tenderly graze her cheek. "You're a good woman, Hannah. You've got a kind heart."

"Sometimes I worry Justin won't ever know his father enough to love or hate him. I can't believe there won't be a price to pay for that, too. But it doesn't have to be that way for C.J."

"I guess it's up to me to see that it isn't."

His words served as his cue to leave. Devin turned away slowly and Hannah followed him onto the porch, intending to call Justin inside. But she hesitated when Devin stopped, facing the bunkhouse where C.J. waited this moment on a call from Jolene that likely wouldn't come. His voice low and filled with regret, Devin said, "It never seems to be the right time for us, Hannah."

Hannah blinked hard against sudden tears, seeking out Justin down the long length of porch. "No, it doesn't," she agreed softly, and Devin walked away.

August gave way to September, bringing the start of school for C.J. Justin was angry that he wasn't old

enough yet to go to school, C.J. sullen because he had
to. Hannah noted that riding the school bus to a
nearby small town with Allie seemed to take out some
of the sting for C.J.

Justin hadn't minded being left behind today. At
Devin's insistence, Hannah had allowed him to stay
home and "help" at the barn while she made a trip
to Greeley for a sonogram. Upon her return, Hannah
noted the day had turned cool. Waving goodbye to
Tilly, who'd accompanied her, she fastened a button
of her long loose jean jacket to ward off the breeze.
She liked the idea of her baby-to-be tucked snug inside the warm denim.

Hannah smiled. Her healthy baby-to-be.

Hannah crossed to the barn to retrieve her son from
underfoot. But the quiet barn seemed empty. Then she
spied the bag of carrots that lay before Jet's open stall
door and planted her hand on her hip. "Justin Reese,
are those my carrots for tomorrow night's stew?"

Three guilty-looking cowboys dressed in varying
shades of blue flannel and denim stepped into the
aisle.

Jet poked his head out the open door, bobbing his
head, his white star flashing. Hannah sighed, the carrots forgotten. It wasn't enough that her son adored
Devin and idolized C.J.; he was crazy about Jet, as
well. Through no fault of Devin's, Justin was coming
to know a sense of family he'd never felt with Travis.
Concern welled up within her, thinking of the void
that would be left in Justin's life once Devin and C.J.
were gone.

"Can I ride out with C.J. to meet Allie?" Justin ran over and clung to her leg, clearly begging, as C.J. resumed saddling the horse.

Hannah's first thought was to refuse; how could spending more time with C.J. help Justin? She doubted that C.J. wanted Justin along, and she wasn't sure it was safe for Justin to ride double on the horse anyway. But before she could think of a way to let Justin down, C.J. muttered from inside the stall, "He can ride, if he wants."

Justin released her, disappearing back into the stall, unaware C.J. sounded reluctant as always. But Hannah sensed an acceptance of sorts in C.J.'s invitation that made it difficult not to let her hopes rise in Devin's direction.

Minutes later, outside the barn, Devin hoisted Justin up behind C.J. and the boys started Jet off at a walk down the fence line. Hannah wrapped her hand around the top rail, gazing after them.

Devin came to stand beside her, taking off his hat and turning it in his hands in a gesture Hannah recognized from the morning she'd overslept. "So, how did the sonogram go?"

He asked the question with the same endearing concern he'd shown that morning. Touched, Hannah responded reassuringly, "The baby's healthy and strong."

"Sounds like a boy."

"I think it's a girl," Hannah said, worrying as Jet bobbed his head in impatience at the slow pace C.J. set.

Devin pushed his hat back on. "You could just let the doctor tell you."

The horse wasn't the only impatient one around here, Hannah thought. "That would be like knowing what the present was before you unwrapped it."

Jet pranced sideways then, and Hannah gripped the rail more tightly.

"Relax. They'll be fine. C.J.'s got a real way with that horse."

"If you're sure…"

"I'm sure, Hannah."

Devin sounded like his usual confident self now. And Devin was right; C.J. had a way with Jet that transformed the high-strung animal into a gentle giant. That C.J. loved Jet was plain, and Hannah said impulsively, "You know, there's no sense in either of us pretending Travis is going to come up with any money for that horse."

"Are you telling me I'm free to sell my horse if I want?" Devin teased dryly.

"I was thinking that you'd let C.J. *have* him," Hannah said tartly.

Devin chuckled. "You're bound and determined to cost me money, woman."

"C.J. needs that horse, Devin!"

"I've been sensing that need in him, same as you," Devin said.

Hannah settled back then, satisfied. But she couldn't help wishing she could fulfill Justin's needs as easily.

"What about the financial speculation you're taking on the horse?'' Devin asked quietly. "Do you plan to take Travis to court after all?''

"No, I won't change my mind about that.''

But she had to come up with some kind of financial plan besides Devin's lease and the horses she now boarded. Her throat tightened at the very thought of him someday leaving. To distract herself, Hannah said, "The guest ranch where Tilly works is expanding their operation. I'm hoping they might have horses to board here.''

"Why not offer them a lease on some land? You wouldn't have to be responsible for their stock then.''

Hannah embraced the idea with excitement. "I have open range that borders the guest ranch. It would be perfect. But I wouldn't know what terms to offer.''

"As I recall, you drive a hard bargain,'' Devin reminded her wryly. Then he grinned at her show of indignation. "I could probably be convinced to offer my expertise on the matter.''

His grin softened and Hannah found that the kiss he stole was enough to persuade him.

And one phone call was all it took to arrange the lease of her land. Hannah found it liberating to know she could get by without Travis's support. That night as she tucked Justin into bed, it was all she could do not to tell him he could count on that pony from Santa for Christmas. Instead, she settled for asking him, "How would you like to go to the toy store next time we're in Greeley?''

"I want to go to the tack shop where C.J. and Devin go,'' Justin said, and Hannah thought she should have expected as much. "I want to buy spurs like Devin's."

"I don't think Jet would like spurs," Hannah said, envisioning a bucking spree. Not to mention the havoc spurs would wreak on her hardwood floors.

"Then I want a big belt buckle."

Like Devin's, it went without saying. Hannah's smile was troubled. "I think Devin wins his buckles at the rodeo, but I suppose we could buy you one."

Justin considered that and decided, "I'll wait and win one when I'm a bronc rider."

Oh, wonderful. "Maybe you'd like a stuffed pony or a belt with Indian beads. Or one of those Pro Rodeo T-shirts like C.J. has. Or maybe—"

"I mostly want a dad."

Hannah's heart missed a beat, a tightness forming in her chest. "You have a father, Justin."

"I mean a real one, like Devin."

A father who cares more for his son than he does the rodeo.

"Your father is…real." Hannah knew her words lacked conviction and she tried to explain. "He's real in the same way C.J.'s mother is real, even though she isn't around all the time."

"C.J.'s mom rides horses." As Justin made that point again, Hannah sighed. Then he added, "But C.J. said it's better to have a mom who makes cookies. He said it takes a lot of time to make cookies."

His words carved a sweet ache in Hannah's heart for both her son and C.J. Trying to cheer Justin up, she told him, "I promise to learn to ride after the baby's born."

"You can ride with me, Mommy."

Hannah leaned down and hugged him, relieved they'd weathered this storm. But as she pulled away she heard Justin whisper, "I still want a dad like Devin."

Justin curled up with his blanket and soft stuffed toys, already half-asleep. Hannah resisted the urge to smooth his dark curls, lest she stir him and start him wishing all over again. She tiptoed across the room and closed the door, leaning back on it with a sense of despair. How ironic that what Justin wanted most of all was something money couldn't buy.

Hannah realized in that moment that all the material gifts her parents had longed to buy her would never have meant as much as the love they'd given. She wanted Justin to know that kind of love, too. Recalling C.J.'s growing acceptance and Devin's kiss, she couldn't help but hope she might someday be able to give Justin the kind of family it seemed they'd both come to dream of.

Chapter Ten

November air sneaked beneath the tent Hannah's jacket formed over her belly and stole through the knit of her ivory sweater. Brown brittle stems of prairie grass snapped beneath her boots. She'd gone out to meet the boys as they rode in on Jet and she walked alongside them now, the horse's hooves raking the grass with a crackling swish that lent vibrancy to the overcast day. Brushing her unbound hair from her cold cheek, Hannah inhaled deeply, her baby stirring inside her as if it enjoyed the brisk outing as much as she.

Justin was having fun, too, he and C.J. wearing their cowboy hats and bundled in new black-and-purple down jackets Devin had bought them at the tack shop in Greeley. Hannah simply hadn't been able to make Justin refuse the gift. And she hadn't the heart anymore to tell Justin he couldn't ride with C.J., who seemed willing enough these days to take him, tolerating Justin's questions in that grudging manner that somehow brought a smile to her lips now.

"Why can't we go fast?" Justin demanded.

"You don't hurry a horse back to the barn. Gets to be a bad habit for them."

"Why can't I ride him myself? I'd go fast."

"That's why you can't." C.J. stopped Jet outside the barn and reached around, catching hold of Justin, who slid down his arm to drop to the ground.

"Why can't I…"

Hannah sighed at her son's persistence, then turned as Devin rolled open the barn door, lean in faded jeans, handsome in a jacket the same shade of gray as his eyes. He looked at his son, then his troubled gaze touched her. He'd heard from Jolene, Hannah was certain. When C.J. led Jet inside, she caught Justin's arm to keep him from following.

"I want to brush Jet." Justin tried to tug free.

"Devin needs to talk to C.J. privately." Devin's low voice drifted to her even as he walked with his son up the aisle to tether the horse in the cross ties. Because Justin's pout warned he was gearing up for a tantrum, Hannah suggested, "Why don't you show me the kittens?"

"Okay."

Justin was always ready to show off the kittens. With his help, Hannah slid the barn door shut, then let Justin lead her to the last stall, empty but for the mama cat and her babies playing and running about her in their fresh bed of straw.

With the awkwardness of any woman eight months pregnant, Hannah knelt to admire the three-month-old kittens, pulling off her gloves and putting them into her coat pocket. Soon, sharp voices drew her back to her feet. Assuring herself Justin was preoccupied with the kittens, she stepped to the stall door just as C.J. jerked free of Devin's placating hand on his shoulder.

For an instant C.J.'s pained gaze met hers. Then bitterness crossed his face and he stormed toward the front of the barn, shoving open the door, pushing his way outside.

Devin threw aside the brush he'd been holding and sent Jet skittering in the cross ties. He stood a moment, his head bowed, his hands fisted at his sides, before settling the horse with a soothing hand on its withers. He sought Hannah out unerringly, and his need beckoned to her. Devin was helpless to ease C.J.'s pain. But she wasn't.

Maybe she couldn't change the way Jolene handled matters. But she could avoid bringing more pain into C.J.'s life. A pain that flashed each time he glimpsed something between her and Devin.

A sense of despair sprang well-deep in Hannah. But through that despair came the realization that she couldn't bear to hurt C.J. any more than she could have hurt Justin. She'd made a place in her heart for C.J., whether he wanted it or not.

"Mommy, can I brush Jet now?" Justin had abandoned the kittens to edge past her into the aisle.

"Devin's putting him in the stall. Why don't you get him some hay to eat?"

"Okay. I'll use my red wagon. Is C.J. going to help me?"

"C.J. went to the bunkhouse for a while. Do you think you can handle the job by yourself?"

Fortunately a sense of responsibility put doing the chore alone in a new light. Justin went off to load his wagon and Hannah walked to Jet's stall.

Devin had turned out the horse into the paddock. Now he leaned in the door of the stall, suddenly aware his problems weren't going to begin and end with C.J. today. Something in the way Hannah looked at him—or rather, looked away from him—served to warn him.

"Jolene called while the boys were riding," he told her. "She won't be coming for C.J. at Thanksgiving."

Hannah released a harsh breath. "How can she hurt him this way again and again?"

Her anger helped to take the edge off his. "Her excuse is the usual, that she's 'busy.' Even C.J. knows by now that means there's another man in his mother's life."

"That's so unfair to C.J.," Hannah said tautly, reflecting a frustration he knew well. That she felt so much for his son warmed Devin's soul. He reached for her, drawing her into the stall, the desire to hold her blooming naturally from that warmth.

Devin gently turned Hannah's back to the wall. He leaned close and her soft roundness brought forth a surge of protectiveness made poignant by the uncertain way she curled her hands on his chest. She drew him with her compassion, yet she held him at bay. Devin feared he knew the reason.

"I should check on Justin. He might be cold."

"Kids don't get cold." Devin let go of her arms and wrapped his hands around Hannah's. Her pulse beat hotly at her wrist, but her skin felt icy. Devin smiled in understanding. "You're the one who's cold."

"I have gloves..."

"I can warm you better." Devin linked his fingers with hers, felt her skin heating against his as he kept their hands close to his chest. "How's that?"

"Warmer," Hannah admitted.

"Your cheeks are cold, too." The frosty air had pinched color onto her ivory face. With his hands already occupied, Devin knew only one way to chase off the chill. He lowered his head to warm Hannah's cheek with his kiss.

Her skin was cool to his lips, sweet to his tongue, and the quick gasp she gave sent him seeking her mouth. Hannah curled her fingers tightly with his and Devin drew as close as the baby would allow. Then she turned her cheek and Devin grazed his mouth across skin he had warmed, the taste bittersweet now.

"I know you want me." Devin breathed the words at her ear in hot frustration, stirring her silky hair.

"No." Hannah drew a ragged breath. "Justin's going to have enough change in his life once this baby's born."

Devin knew her heart wasn't in her words. He released her and placed his hands on her belly. Even through her coat, he could feel the baby shift strongly inside her, as if it shared his impatience. This child was already more his than Travis's, and Devin let possessiveness deepen his voice as he told her, "I want to be a part of that change, Hannah."

Tears shone in Hannah's eyes. But she caught his hands in hers and shifted away. Devin was certain it was for the sake of his son. Only the fact that he needed to do the same kept him from stopping her as she walked out of the stall.

As he followed, closing the stall door, Hannah asked, "Please tell C.J. I appreciate him taking Justin riding."

Then, unexpectedly, Justin called C.J.'s name from the haystack. Pivoting, Devin realized his son was there. He exchanged a quick frown with Hannah, wondering when C.J. had come back into the barn.

"C.J.! Catch me!"

C.J. half turned in response to Justin. And Devin saw the metal prongs of the pitchfork gleaming upright in C.J.'s hand. Saw his son unaware of Justin's intent.

His blood ran cold. The warning burst from his lungs. "C.J.!"

"Justin!" The cry was Hannah's as Justin launched himself from the hay.

Devin sprinted toward them. The clatter of the fork to the aisle was a sound he would hear to the end of his days. He halted, his eyes riveted on the boys. As Hannah ran up behind him, he spun instinctively to catch her.

Hannah fought off his hands, shoved at him with a force that staggered Devin. Her sob tore at his heart. "Justin!"

"He's all right." Devin's voice sounded like gravel even to his own ears. "Slow down now." He loosened his grip on Hannah's arm, turning her to where his son awkwardly clutched Justin to his chest. Justin had wound his arms about C.J.'s neck, and his dark curls shone in the rays that beamed through the skylight, his lost hat the only concession to his leap from the haystack. C.J.'s face was the color of chalk, his eyes huge and dark.

Hannah covered her mouth with her hands. Devin felt her knees buckle and he shored her up, though he was feeling weak-kneed himself as they headed down the aisle.

C.J. stood rooted, while Justin squirmed, wanting down, oblivious to his near mishap. There was no mistaking the heartfelt squeeze C.J. gave Justin before he relinquished the boy to Devin. As Devin deposited Justin within reach of Hannah's waiting arms, he asked, "You okay, son?"

"I almost killed him," C.J. whispered hoarsely.

"You shouldn't be carrying around the fork with the prongs up, especially with a little tyke around," Devin conceded. Then he rested his hand reassuringly on C.J.'s shoulder, a gesture he seemed to call on often of late. "But you thought fast, son. You kept Justin from getting hurt."

C.J. appeared to accept that, if only because he couldn't bear not to.

Justin listened solemnly as Hannah pointed out the pitchfork. But when he failed to appreciate Hannah's efforts to fuss over him, pulling free to hide out in the stall with the kittens, Hannah turned her attention to C.J.

"I'm sorry Justin gave you such a scare. If you hadn't reacted so quickly…" She shuddered, clearly unable to go on. She reached out to touch C.J.'s arm. "Are *you* all right?"

Devin frowned as C.J. shrugged, trying, but failing to break contact with Hannah. "I'm okay."

"Are you sure? Justin gave you little warning—"

"I said I'm okay! Just leave me alone!" C.J. jerked free and stalked off.

"C.J., what's wrong?" As Hannah moved instinctively after him, Devin caught her arm.

"Let him go. C.J. blames himself, that's all. He'll see reason after he has time to mull things over."

"I don't think that's it." Hannah winced when C.J. sent the barn door rattling on its runners. "He doesn't want my gratitude any more than he wants my blame." Softly she added, "I can only hurt him now."

Hannah moved away, going into the stall to retrieve Justin while the truth of her words set in for Devin.

Before leaving, Justin caught Devin in a quick embrace, innocent of the fright he'd given them. Devin was certain Hannah would further enlighten her son to the dangers of leaping from the haystack. And he desperately wanted the right to teach Justin alongside her, to act as a father to Justin and a husband to Hannah.

Alone, Devin went to the back barn door, giving it a shove, letting the cold seep past the open edges of his jacket. He tried to shake off a mood gone gray as the cloudy sky.

He knew that what was between him and Hannah was right. He loved her—and Justin and the baby.

And there was no doubt in his mind that C.J. and Justin had come to be like brothers. C.J. had settled in here and at school, his friendship with Allie growing. All of this in spite of himself. C.J. still denied himself the attention Hannah offered. But Hannah cared about C.J., and Devin had to believe that his son would eventually return those feelings.

Because he didn't know what he would do if C.J. couldn't accept Hannah having a role in their lives.

Chapter Eleven

Devin had insisted on driving them all to Denver for Thanksgiving. But Hannah had spent the day with Justin at her parents' home, while Devin and C.J. had gone on to his sister's. The separation was what she'd wanted, what was for the best. Yet it simply hadn't felt right to her.

Now, with Thanksgiving a bittersweet memory, Hannah gazed out the kitchen window. The winter sky was as heavy with snow as she felt weighed down with child, and she wondered what Christmas would bring. The holiday was less than three weeks away, her cesarean section scheduled three days from now. She'd arranged for Tilly to care for Justin. Devin had offered, but she'd politely refused. Somehow that hadn't felt right, either.

The boys were making their way toward the house after late-day chores at the barn. Envying their agility as they bent to pet the mama cat, Hannah rubbed the aching small of her back through her sweater in unconscious imitation of Devin. She thought wistfully that his touch had changed of late. It was soothing. Relaxing. Downright asexual. That upset her, despite the fact that she felt asexual herself these days. Though she'd been the one to turn him away, it hurt to think that maybe Devin no longer wanted her, the way Travis had stopped wanting her.

Still, Devin had taken her and the boys to the foothills to find a tree for Christmas, which was more than Travis had ever done. They'd returned as the first round of the National Finals Rodeo in Las Vegas aired on TV, and they'd watched while they set up the tree. The boys were certain Devin would have had a shot at the all-round championship had he been there, and Devin hadn't bothered to refute them, his longing to compete obvious. Hannah had easily pictured herself there with the boys and even her baby, cheering him on the way she had at Cheyenne. The way Tilly said it could be....

Travis hadn't made the finals and Hannah hadn't missed his presence in her living room via TV. But C.J. clearly missed his mother's absence in the barrel race. He'd excused himself, and Devin had followed. Hannah had watched the remaining nights of rodeo with Justin.

The tramp of the boys' boots on the porch had Hannah turning to the door. Justin burst inside, pulling at the zipper of his jacket, C.J. stepping in behind him and closing the door. She'd gotten in the habit of having hot chocolate waiting along with C.J.'s cookies and pay.

"Mommy, we're hungry. Devin told us to go on up to the house." Justin tugged at his gloves. C.J. followed suit so naturally, so much as if he belonged here, that Hannah's heart warmed. Then, as if remembering some part in a play, he seemed to deliberately summon a wall around him.

The telephone rang and Hannah lifted the receiver, still pondering C.J.'s behavior as she said automatically, "Reese Ranch. Hannah speaking."

"This is Jolene."

Hannah stiffened, a fierce protectiveness rising within her.

"I need to talk to C.J., but Dev isn't answering. Any chance you know where they are?"

Hannah wanted to deny it. But, ignoring the sarcasm laced through Jolene's query, she made herself reply, "C.J. happens to be right here." Hannah loosened her fist from around the cord and reluctantly held out the receiver to C.J. "Your mother would like to speak with you."

Hannah didn't imagine C.J.'s wariness as he took the call. He turned away, shoving his free hand in his jacket pocket as he mumbled, "Mom?"

Hannah pressed a finger to her lips to keep Justin silent, but he didn't seem to notice. He was listening somberly on his own, C.J.'s mother having come to represent a threat to his happiness.

"But you promised. You said I could go with you at Christmas!" There was a bitter bite to C.J.'s words that stemmed from the pain of another promise being broken. Hannah wanted to take back the phone, to spare him somehow. But C.J. listened only a moment longer before drawing a harsh breath to claim, "You don't want me at all!"

C.J. slammed down the phone as Devin walked in the door, taking grim stock of the situation. Justin reached out to curl his small hand into the hem of C.J.'s jacket, but C.J., shrouded in hurt, didn't seem to notice.

Hannah's heart broke for C.J. On impulse she invited, "Have Christmas with us. Justin would love it."

"You don't mean that." C.J.'s eyes blazed accusingly. "You don't want more change in Justin's life."

Her own words lashed her as C.J. shoved past Devin and out the door. Hannah barely noticed Justin race out on C.J.'s heels as realization blossomed through her pain.

C.J. had overheard her and Devin that day in the barn before Justin's mishap. C.J. thought she had no room for him in her and Justin's lives.

"That's it." His jaw set, Devin turned toward the door as it settled in his son's wake. Hannah grabbed her jacket to follow, but hearing her, Devin spun back to stop her. "Hold on now. You don't need to be out in this cold."

"I have to talk to C.J.," Hannah insisted. "I've hurt him, the same as Jolene."

She feared he would argue, but Devin took her jacket and helped her into it. Hannah fidgeted with impatience, then embarrassment, as he tugged the buttons snugly closed over her belly, nothing amorous in his touch to reassure her that he still wanted her.

"Let's go." Devin's impatience matched hers as they stepped onto the porch. But the boys were nowhere in sight.

When Devin aimed for the bunkhouse, Hannah caught his arm. "I think C.J. and Justin might be with Jet."

"You're probably right." Devin hesitated, then advised her, "Head on over to the barn. I'll check out the bunkhouse real quick, just in case."

Before striding off, he gave her hand a squeeze that Hannah tried not to read too much into, even as she folded her fingers to hold in the warmth of his touch.

She walked to the barn, conscious of her back aching and a quickening low in her belly, as if the baby sensed her urgency despite her careful pace. She couldn't bear to think she'd hurt C.J. Small wonder the boy had remained so determined not to like her. But his hurt had proved one thing: he cared what she thought about him, meaning he did have some regard for her. She was anxious to set C.J. straight.

But once she'd slipped inside the barn, Hannah paused. As anticipated, she could hear the boys down the aisle in the stall with Jet, Justin earnest as always, C.J. murmuring back, calmer now. Hannah smiled gently. Justin, in all his innocence, might smooth the way for them all.

For a moment Hannah's hopes rose. If C.J. came to accept the truth about Jolene, if she could make him understand that she hadn't meant to hurt him, there was nothing to keep them from being a family— unless Devin truly no longer wanted her and saw only himself and C.J. free to return to life on the rodeo circuit.

The churn of wheels came from the gravel lane, then the sound of a rig pulling up. Hannah stepped back outside the door and groaned. It was Travis, with his red horse trailer hitched to the new truck he'd bought himself after the divorce. He didn't seem to notice her as he climbed out the far side, pulling on an expensive sheepskin-lined leather jacket. Of all times for Travis to show up. Well, if he still wanted Jet he was out of luck, Hannah thought with satisfaction. The horse was C.J.'s now.

Devin strode over from the bunkhouse as the first flakes of snow fell, dusting the shoulders of his gray jacket. He pushed up his hat brim and eyed Travis boldly, stopping directly before him with no regard for the fact that Travis had knocked him out last time they met. There was an edge to his voice as he confirmed, "If you've come for the horse, Reese, I could have saved you a trip. Jet isn't for sale anymore."

Hannah held her breath, waiting for Travis's reply.

"Maybe I came to see my boy." Hannah could hear the grin in Travis's voice, and her breath hissed out in a frosty vapor that sent descending snowflakes swirling. He didn't really want to see Justin at all. Then her heart stopped in its beat as Travis went on, "I've got some time coming with Justin. Thought I'd take him with me for a while."

No! Hannah's throat grew tight, her breath shored in her lungs. She backed up a step, instinctively blocking the open section of barn door. She wanted Travis to get to know his son, but he couldn't just suddenly take Justin, no matter what the terms of the divorce granted. The sad truth was, Justin wouldn't want to go with his father.

"The boy hardly knows you." Devin echoed her thoughts, his voice hard. In that moment Hannah knew he would never let Travis take Justin with him.

"I've got a legal right to my son. You know all about those legal rights, don't you, Dev?" Travis's goading chuckle had Hannah curling her hands into fists.

"Justin is more mine than he ever was yours." Devin spoke past gritted teeth. "So is Hannah."

Mine. As if she belonged to him. As if he wanted her. Hannah's future seemed to crystallize with the word. She and Devin, the boys and the baby...

"I kind of figured that was the way of things." Travis spit on the ground. "Doesn't change the law or my plans any. Although—" Travis paused for effect now "—I might be swayed by the offer of a good roping horse. Wouldn't have much time for the boy if I was busy winning trophy buckles on that flashy gelding of yours."

Travis was blackmailing Devin with her son.

The scrape of a boot from behind her had Hannah turning. C.J. stood at the door, his glare aimed at Travis. Justin came running up beside him, and C.J. caught hold of his arm, keeping him back. Away from his father. Hannah's heart squeezed as she heard Devin say, "Take the horse and get out of here, Reese."

Hannah could stand no more. Travis wasn't getting away with this. She took a bold step forward, faltering when that quickening in her belly came again, more pronounced. More like a contraction....

Hannah clutched at her belly. That just couldn't be. She breathed deeply, the cold air bracing her. It was just all this tension... Devin looked her way then, and the angry gaze he'd had for Travis turned to one of question. Hannah deliberately lowered her hands to her sides, trying to ignore the twinges racing across her abdomen as she crossed toward the men.

"How dare you come here making threats, Travis Reese."

"I've got rights, Hannah. If I want the boy—"

"You're not taking Justin anywhere," Devin ground out, then they all stilled as the sound of hoofbeats out back of the barn sifted through the snowy cold air.

Hannah gripped Devin's arm. "C.J. overheard Travis. He must have taken Jet."

Travis made a sound of disgust. "That little son of a—"

Devin jerked free of her grasp and landed a solid blow with his fist to Travis's solar plexus. Travis hit the ground on his knees, clutching his middle as he gasped for air.

Hannah gasped, too, but her dismay was due more to the mild contraction that seized her as Devin caught hold of her arms to demand, "Was Justin with C.J.?"

"Yes." Recalling the protective way C.J. had held back Justin, panic skittered through Hannah. C.J. would no more let Travis take Justin than the horse. There hadn't been time to saddle Jet, and the thought of the boys riding bareback over slick snowy ground had her heart pounding.

"I'll bring them back safely," Devin promised. And he planted a firm kiss on her mouth that eased Hannah right through the contraction. "Why don't you get the hell out of here, Reese," he suggested, then strode to his pickup, getting in and gunning the engine, wheeling toward the back of the barn.

"That son of a bitch."

Travis staggered to his feet, referring to Devin this time, Hannah thought wryly. She raked her gaze with disgust from his hat of Triple X Beaver to his fancy leather coat to the expensive lizard-skin boots he wore.

"I want you off this ranch, Travis Reese."

"Now wait just a minute—"

"You're going to forget all about taking our son or that horse, or I'll see you in jail over child support."

"You wouldn't do that," Travis blustered.

"I wouldn't have. Now I will." The truth of it saddened her, and it brought a wariness to Travis's gaze. "You'd better change your ways, Travis. Justin won't be a child forever. Someday he's going to know you for the man you are. So will this baby."

She left him then and went to grasp the fence and watch through falling snow for Devin and the boys, grateful she'd quit crying over Travis months ago.

But a hot tear slipped down her cold cheek for Justin when she heard Travis pull out in his rig, not even waiting to see his son brought back safely.

Hannah's next contraction proved strong enough to divert her. She was relieved when Devin drove into view, C.J. and Justin riding alongside on Jet.

Devin braked and climbed from the truck, waving the boys on into the barn. His first thought was, at least that bastard, Reese, was gone. The boys were safe and the four of them—*five,* he amended with a grin, thinking of the baby—were going to sit down and have a long talk about becoming a family.

Then he turned and saw Hannah, standing at the fence, her left hand wrapped around the top rail, her right clutching her belly. She smiled at him gratefully. Weakly. *Clutching her belly...*

"Dear God..." Devin prayed with a mix of elation and fear. The baby was coming.

Chapter Twelve

Justin came really fast...

So much damage...

Hannah's words came back to haunt Devin as he held Justin close, the boy asleep on his lap in a waiting-room chair at Greeley's North Colorado Medical Center.

What if it happens again?

What if something happens to Hannah or the baby?

He'd take care of Justin always. *But please, God, don't let anything happen—*

"Dad?"

C.J.'s voice brought a halt to Devin's rampant thoughts as his son shifted in the chair beside him.

C.J. pushed up his hat brim, revealing his troubled gray eyes. That he'd come to care about Hannah was clear as he asked uncertainly, "Is she going to be all right?"

"Hannah will be fine, son." *Please, God, let her be fine.* Hoping to reassure both C.J. and himself, he added, "She'll need our help after the baby comes."

"That's not what she said that day in the barn when you kissed her."

"Hannah's trying not to hurt you. She knows how much you love and miss your mother."

"Yeah. I miss Mom just like Mom misses me," C.J. said scathingly. But there were tears in C.J.'s eyes that told Devin Hannah had been right; C.J. couldn't hate his mother.

And he didn't want C.J. to. "She's the one who stopped needing us, C.J. That doesn't mean you can't still love her."

"*You* don't still love her," C.J. pointed out ruthlessly.

Not since she hurt you. "I'm trying to forgive her and get on with my life. That's what you need to do, too."

C.J. was left to mull that over when the doctor approached, bringing Devin to his feet. Justin stirred in sleep to cling to his neck. Devin wanted to ask after Hannah, but the words wouldn't come past the tightness in his throat.

"A healthy baby girl, seven pounds and an ounce. Mother is tired, but doing fine." The robust doctor made his announcement as if there'd been no reason to expect anything else.

A little girl...

"You were able to do the cesarean?" Devin managed to ask hoarsely.

"You got her here just in time. Although…" The doctor cocked his head. "Are you family of Hannah's?"

"I'm going to be," Devin said determinedly.

"I see." A nurse was waving the doctor on to another delivery and he said hurriedly, "I'll be back to speak with her as soon as I can. Maybe you'd like to go see her and the baby?"

"God, yes." Devin shared a look of relief with C.J., hugging Justin tightly enough to fully wake him.

It seemed he'd waited an eternity to see Hannah; but time stopped for him when he stepped over the threshold and into her room. He drew a quick breath past the knot in his throat and knew he would never forget the way Hannah looked to him in this moment. So very tired, so fragile. And yet so very beautiful and strong.

Her curls were caught loosely in a band to spill over her shoulder, her eyes dark stars in the heaven of her pale face, shining down on the baby she cradled protectively in her arms.

"Mommy?" Justin spoke past a yawn.

Hannah looked up then and smiled. Hat in hand, Devin stood in the doorway, his black hair sweeping across his forehead, the shadow of a beard darkening his jaw. He held her sleepy son on one arm, his own son standing beside him. She would never forget the way he looked to her in that moment, strong and masculine, yet utterly weary, the vulnerable light in his smoky eyes attesting to the fright she'd given him.

Justin rubbed his eyes with his small curled knuckles. C.J. hovered uncertainly. Hannah beckoned them over, wanting to comfort Justin and to reassure C.J. But it was Devin who captured her attention first as he deposited Justin carefully beside her on the bed, then brushed a gentle kiss on her cheek.

"The doctor said he'd be in to talk to you." Devin stole another quick kiss that Hannah hoped hid her apprehension. The cesarean had gone perfectly. But all that bearing down beforehand...

"Is that my brother?" Justin demanded.

"This is your *sister*." Hannah willed her dark thoughts away. She glanced sheepishly at Devin. "I can't seem to decide on a name for her."

Devin touched one finger to the sleeping baby's cap of soft dark hair. "She looks like you. How about Anna? Sort of like Hannah, yet her own name."

"Anna. I like that." And she loved the way he gently touched her child, loved the way he looked at her and her baby, his eyes full of pride and possession. With that love welling inside her, she asked, "What do you boys think?"

C.J. tried to act nonchalant, but he took a moment to consider before he decided. "Sounds okay."

"Hi, Anna." Justin peered down into the baby's face, squinting and wrinkling his nose in imitation of hers. "She looks kind of funny." Then he sweetly kissed Anna's forehead, apparently willing to overlook that she wasn't a boy.

"She's very special," Hannah said softly. "Just like you boys."

Secure in that knowledge, Justin only tried to convince Anna to open her eyes. But C.J. said quietly, with no trace of grudge in his voice, "Thanks."

"You can ride horses now, Mommy." Justin reminded her, his usual doggedness making them laugh.

"As soon as I can," Hannah vowed, though the very thought made her wince. She couldn't remember when she'd last been so sore. Or so happy. The five of them here together was all she could have wished for.

But Devin seemed to think it was time for the visit to end.

"C.J., why don't you take Justin and round up a snack while you wait for Tilly?"

Justin hugged her then as if she was made of glass, as if he'd been coached to "handle with care," Hannah thought, smiling. C.J. touched Anna's small foot before leaving, the gesture all the more endearing coming from a thirteen-year-old boy.

"Tilly's going to take the boys on back to the ranch," Devin explained once they'd gone. Then he went on huskily, "But if it's all right with you, C.J. and I would like to watch over Justin until you get home."

"I'd like that just fine," Hannah said almost shyly, knowing Tilly would be happy about that meaningful turn of events. It felt right to know Devin would take care of Justin, take care of everything....

Hannah realized then how late it was, how tired

she was. And she was suddenly struck by how close she'd come to having this baby at the ranch. As she held Anna close, tears burned her eyes and she shuddered with delayed reaction. "If you hadn't been there today—"

"Shh..." Devin gently scooped Anna from her arms. "Justin would have managed to call Tilly. You would have been fine." He rocked the baby, somehow soothing Hannah in the process. "I should have expected this of Annie. She had an impatient kick."

Annie. A pet name, like a father would give a daughter. Fresh tears filled Hannah's eyes.

"Ah, Hannah. Don't cry. Everything turned out fine. Close your eyes now."

She did, because she couldn't seem to stop crying while she watched him hold Annie like she was his own. "I'm just so happy."

"I know you are." She felt his smile as Devin pressed his lips to her temple. "Dream good dreams." To her cheek. "Dream about us." To the corner of her mouth. "Dream about more children..."

But Hannah slept dreamlessly. And when morning came she learned that this time there was absolutely no chance of another child.

I always wanted more kids....

The words Devin had once spoken to her haunted Hannah.

It was almost Christmas.

A frosty layer of snow had fallen during the night and the morning was fresh with it, the boys making tracks as they tended to chores. Devin watched them from outside the bunkhouse door, the glare of early sun in his eyes, his coffee gone cold in the cup in his hand. His thoughts were on Hannah. Hannah nursing Annie, changing Annie, rocking Annie…

He told himself she was withdrawn because she was busy with the baby, because she needed rest. She hadn't slept well during her stay at the hospital. But while Hannah had been home a week now, the time never seemed right to have that talk about becoming a family.

He'd wanted them to be married by now. Sharing the same tree on Christmas morning. Sharing the same bed at night.

Devin scrubbed his hand down his face. In the days before Annie had been born, his hormones had gone strangely dormant, his thoughts constantly on the baby-to-be, almost as if he was the one who was pregnant. He'd been content to rub Hannah's back, and at the time, that had made it easier to do what was best for C.J.

But what was best for C.J. had changed. And Devin's hormones were now functioning at peak performance, awaiting Hannah's return to health. But while he knew she wanted him, too, he was fighting a growing fear that this change in her was permanent, that she'd changed her mind about making a place for him in her life.

He would do anything for Hannah. Devin swept the ranch with his gaze. It hadn't taken long to figure out that for Hannah, child support had become no more than a means to keep Travis in line. She'd get by on her leases, but with the sale of some horses he could go ahead and make this ranch hers, the way she dreamed of. He'd teach her to ride. He'd make sure she loved the rodeo or he'd give it up. Whatever she wanted he'd give her—be it the ranch, horses, more children...

Children.

Devin's heart stilled.

Hannah hadn't expected to have another child after Justin, who had come too fast. Annie had come along like a miracle. Devin saw her as a miracle in his life, too.

But Annie had also come too fast.

His heart drummed a painful beat. Hannah's cesarean had been successful. But instead of happy, she'd been withdrawn.

There could be only one reason. The pain in his heart seemed to swell as he realized that Annie was going to be her last child. She'd kept it from him, but he should have known, should have seen how she was hurting.

His thoughts had been centered on Hannah, the baby and the boys as he'd envisioned them as a family. But he hadn't known how strongly that vision had come to include giving Hannah another baby.

Now he understood that Annie would be his last child, too. Now he knew how Hannah was hurting.

The sun seemed suddenly overbright, making his eyes burn. The cold reached achingly deep inside him.

He knew there would always be a place in his heart for the child that would never be.

Devin set his cup on a window ledge. He started toward the house, breaking through crisp snow with each boot step. Climbing the porch steps, he moved out of the blinding sun. In answer to his knock on the door, Hannah bid him to come in out of the cold.

He heard the creak of the rocker as he opened the door. Devin crossed the kitchen slowly, stepping into the patch of sunlight that poured over Hannah as she sat by the window, her dark hair lying in waves on the shoulders of her pink pajamas. Annie slept serenely in her arms. There was milk on the baby's rosy mouth, her eyes lacy black crescents above her round pink cheeks.

"She's beautiful, Hannah. *You're* beautiful."

Hannah stopped rocking as she watched Devin sweep off his hat, his black hair falling over his forehead as he knelt before her.

He knew. She saw that the hurt she'd been holding inside now darkened his smoky eyes.

She'd wanted to be brave, to be noble and not hold on to Devin when she learned she could give him no children. But somehow she was crying, and Devin was pulling her up, holding her. She pressed her cheek to the familiar soft denim beneath his jacket, with Annie cradled like something precious and rare between them.

It was warmer this way, with Devin's arms around her, the sun shining in over the three of them. She turned her head and could see the boys out the window, flinging snowballs in front of the barn. *Let this be enough,* Hannah thought.

"I'm sorry, Hannah."

She closed her eyes, as if she could shut out the pain his words would bring if he didn't love her, didn't want the family she believed they'd become.

"I can't think of anything on earth I'd rather have given you than another child."

Hannah's breath caught in her throat. The sun stayed warm on her face and bright against her lowered lashes. She felt that warmth and light reach inside her and bloom in her heart as hope; the hope that Devin still wanted her in spite of everything.

"But we've all got a need for each other. C.J. needs a mother, Justin and Annie a father."

Hannah opened her eyes, loving him.

"I need you, Hannah," Devin whispered. "We'll share the regret, and Annie and the boys will be all the more special for it."

Wistful now, she told him, "I wanted to carry a baby for you."

"And so you have." Devin kissed her gently. Then, careful of Annie, he kissed her in earnest, until she had no doubt that he wanted her and this family and the life they could have here together.

"And to think just before Annie was born, I was afraid your desire had waned," Hannah said breathlessly.

"Before Annie was born, my sex drive *did* wane," Devin muttered. Then he added, "But I'm not pregnant anymore," and bent his head to kiss her again, until, realizing what he'd meant, Hannah drew back, laughing. As he held her, a tenderness coming into his eyes, embracing her in its spell, she knew what could make their happiness complete.

"Last night, I dreamed a rodeo cowboy asked me to marry him. A rodeo *champion*," she emphasized, just to be sure he understood. "I know you love me and the children. But I want you to live the life you love, too."

"It's a good dream. That's what the dream catcher's for." Devin cupped her cheek with his hand, loving her. "Will you marry me, Hannah? Will you share that dream with me?"

"Yes, I'll marry you, Devin."

And she knew that this time around it would be different; the love would last. All it took was the right cowboy.

* * * * *

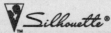

Take 2 bestselling love stories FREE

Plus get a FREE surprise gift!

#1 *New York Times* bestselling author

NORA ROBERTS

**Presents a brand-new book in the
beloved MacGregor series:**

THE WINNING HAND
(SSE#1202)

October 1998 in

Silhouette®SPECIAL EDITION®

Innocent Darcy Wallace needs Mac Blade's protection in
the high-stakes world she's entered. But who will protect
Mac from the irresistible allure of this vulnerable beauty?

**Coming in March, the much-anticipated novel,
THE MACGREGOR GROOMS
Also, watch for the MacGregor stories
where it all began!**

**December 1998:
THE MACGREGORS: Serena—Caine**

**February 1999:
THE MACGREGORS: Alan—Grant**

**April 1999:
THE MACGREGORS: Daniel—Ian**

Available at your favorite retail outlet, only from

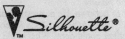

Silhouette
ROMANCE™

COMING NEXT MONTH